Trouble Looming

The Tapestry Series
Book 2

By Natalie Alder

To Jackie ~
Welcome to the
world of the packer
men
Natalie Alder

TROUBLE LOOMING
All rights reserved.
Copyright 2015 © Natalie Alder

Cover by Jo-Anna with Just write. Creations

Cole Becker helped his father raise his younger siblings after their mother died.
He helped his father take care of his aging parents until they passed away.
Now it's time for Cole to have the life he deserves. When he meets Sara, all of his dreams seem to finally be within reach…until things begin to fall apart. Their perfect romance soon becomes complicated, scary, even life-threatening. Will happiness ever be theirs? Will Cole and Sara get their 'someday' together? Continue Tapestry, the Becker's family saga in Trouble Looming, sequel to Crewel Work.

Part One

Cole Becker loved his wife. That wasn't the problem. It was his mother-in-law he didn't care for. And not in the stereotypical my-mother-in-law drives me crazy kind of way. Cole couldn't say he really knew his mother-in-law. She had been severely ill before he even met her daughter. It was the way she had been behind every irritating stumbling block that he'd come up against in life since he met his wife. If Cole hadn't seen the true love his parents had and hadn't witnessed the true love as it grew between his younger sister and her now husband, he probably wouldn't have stood by Sara Thompkins, nor made her his wife. She was truly the woman of his dreams. She was everything he had ever thought a woman he'd like to spend his life with was. She completed him. Sara was everything to him.

Cole knew she was pretty special from the moment he first laid eyes on her. The first time he ever saw her, he had looked down—Sara was five foot two inches tall to Cole's six foot four inches of height—to see her standing near him. Her wet blouse was very see-through, affording him a no-need-to-imagine view of her generous breasts nestled in a lovely pink lace bra. She had silky blonde hair that flowed over her shoulders, expressive deep blue eyes, and curves that didn't quit. But for Cole, that wasn't all he saw. She had treated the incident the evening they first met as it was, an accident, and didn't let it ruin her evening. So many women would have made a whole lot of fuss, yelling and cursing him out, worrying about their hair and makeup. Not Sara. Cole had been impressed.

So, what had happened?
March 2010

Every year Cole, his friend, Jeff Kearny, and their old college buddies who were still living in the Greenville, South Carolina area would meet at the same local Irish pub for their St. Patrick's Day party.

That year, it started out like this. In February, Cole played a round of golf with Jeff. This wasn't unusual since Cole lived about a half an hour drive from Greenville in a small town called Carnegie in the foothills of the Smokey Mountains. He usually called Jeff for a game of golf when Cole was going to be in Greenville for business. Business was working with his father and brother on his family's race horse farm, Bridgeton Pass Farm. He was looking forward to the diversion with his friend since Cole had recently broken up with his girlfriend of the past year and a half, Laurie Drury. He was having trouble with the fact that he kept waiting for the hurt to come after their breakup but it never seemed to happen. He was beginning to think that what he really missed, rather than Laurie, was a soft body to love and someone to laugh with.

"So, you broke it off with Laurie, huh?" Jeff threw the comment out between them to get a feel for whether Cole wanted to talk about it or just play golf and forget about it.

"Yup. Done. Gone. Amazingly, I don't really miss her." Cole wore a half smile.

"Never really could see the two of you together for the long haul."

"No, I guess it never was any great relationship." He watched as his putt sank easily into the hole.

"You cheat, Becker," Jeff whined. Jeff was a software developer. He was plain looking, short, and slightly overweight. He also wasn't very good at golf. Cole usually didn't have much of a problem beating Jeff in a game, but the two enjoyed the occasional opportunity to hang out together.

"No, you just stink at golf." Cole slid his putter into his golf bag.

"You're too honest for your own good. Would you like me to come up with an excuse as to why I can't come out here with you the next time you're in town?"

"You're brilliant at golf, Jeff. I'd have to say you're probably the most talented golf player I know," Cole lied in an effort to save face so that he would continue to have a golf partner in the future.

Jeff laughed. "Will you be in Greenville for St. Patty's Day?" he asked as he set up for his putt.

"You bet. Wouldn't miss it. Speaking of missing it..." Cole watched Jeff's ball roll across the green nowhere near the intended hole.

Cole and Jeff's friends, Bob and Dan, arrived at the Irish pub in Greenville on St. Patrick's Day at three in the afternoon to assure they got a table. That was the excuse they gave, at least, for getting there that early. Signs of typical Irish sayings and prints of Ireland's landscape decorated the pub. It was a decent place that served the college crowd in the area primarily. Meaning the bar was bigger than the dining room and served lots of beer. When Cole walked in at around six o'clock that evening, his friends had already drunk a good amount of green beer. Bob had sidled up to Cole, put his arm around Cole's shoulders and held a beer bottle in front of Cole's face as if it were a microphone. He attempted to lead Cole into singing a traditional Irish drinking song with him. Bob sang out of tune while spitting saliva with every word he attempted to emphasize and his body swaying. Cole was pretty certain the swaying was not an effort to set the rhythm for the song but a result of too much green beer. Cole slid from Bob's arm that had been strewn across his shoulders and went to the bar for a beer. He knew he would need several beers before he would enjoy singing and swaying along with his friend, Bob.

Cole returned to his friends' table with a pitcher. He set it in the middle of the table after he poured himself a pint.

"Shove over," he said to Jeff.

"Ain't nowhere to shove to." Jeff looked at Cole questioningly.

Just then Dan got up from their table to snag a girl for a dance.

"Okay, now shove over." Cole heard Jeff mumble something under his breath as Jeff slid down on the bench seat, making room for Cole to sit. Bob was a chemist and worked for a pharmaceutical company, and Dan was an accountant. The four guys met while in college and had maintained contact since.

"Got your eye on anyone?" Cole asked.

Jeff hadn't had any long term relationships. He wasn't a great conversationalist, worked a lot and had few interests. He was lucky if he could keep a girl's interest for more than one or two dates.

"I asked the brunette with the big green bows on her pigtails to dance, but she turned me down," Jeff admitted reluctantly.

"That's it? You've been here how many hours, and she's the only one you've tried to scoop?" Cole shook his head in disgust.

"I'm still trying to get over Bowie's rejection." Jeff was referring to the girl with the big green bows on her pigtails. "Give me time."

Cole leaned forward and pointed to a group of girls in one corner of the room. "The cute one, next to the girl with the flashing 'Kiss me, I'm Irish' pin on her chest, go now."

"Oh no, Cole…"

"Shut up," Cole said as he stood and pulled Jeff to standing, then pushed him in the direction of the girls.

Cole poured himself another pint and watched Jeff at work. He winced as Jeff stuffed his hands into the front pockets of his jeans and held his shoulders up around his ears. His body language was clear that he lacked self-confidence. Cole wasn't surprised to see the girl shake her head 'no' while her friends looked on, disgust on their faces. Jeff shuffled back to the table with his head down, then fell onto to bench beside Cole.

"Happy now, Becker?" Jeff whined.

"No. Not at all. You should have seen yourself. Where's you mojo, Jeff?"

"My what? Mojo?"

Bob and Dan were now sitting across from them at their table. They both laughed.

"Yeah, Jeff, pull out you mojo!" Dan added. "Be suave or whatever your thing is. You look like a limp fish asking a girl to dance."

"My thing? I don't have a 'thing'!"

"Well, get one," Bob commanded and tried to bang his fist on the table for emphasis. Alcohol thwarted Bob's effort.

Dan righted the empty mug Bob just knocked over. "Yeah, Jeff, come on lure them with your southern gentlemanly manners or pay them flowery compliments. Play up a super power that makes you unique, your thing." Dan drew out the last word.

"Like a cartoon super hero? Are you thinking I need to wear tights and have a cape, 'cause I'm not doin' it."

"Not tonight." Cole brought Jeff back on track. "Tell that brunette in the corner you like her springy shamrock thing on her head. She'll love that you noticed it."

"What's wrong with you, dude? Don't you have any sisters?" Bob asked.

"No." Jeff got up from his seat.

"Take your hands out of your pockets!" Cole instructed at the last minute.

Jeff gave Cole the finger behind his back as he walked away and went over to the brunette in the corner.

Dan, Bob, and Cole watched as the brunette smiled, bounced a little, then let Jeff lead her onto the dance floor. Green beer sloshed over their table as the guys toasted Jeff's success with their pints.

"Third time's a charm," Dan pointed out.

By ten o'clock that evening the place became so packed it was difficult to move. Cole was somewhat surprised that it was that packed given it was a Tuesday night. He decided he'd allow himself one more beer, then planned on waiting until about eleven o'clock to leave before driving.

"This pitcher's on me, guys," Cole told his friends as he got up and left their table.

"Becker's the balls!" Jeff yelled at hearing Cole was buying.

Cole smiled at his ridiculous friends and made his way through the tight crowd to the bar. He was forced to wait at one point for a waiter to finish setting down a tray of pitchers and mugs for a table of sorority girls. While he was standing and waiting, a slim hand slid under the back of his T-shirt and reached around to feel his abs. Reflexively, Cole's stomach muscles tightened. Her touch was light enough and unexpected that it tickled at first. He looked down and gave her a sexy grin, then let her fingers explore his torso while he stood there waiting. Just as he stepped away from the table of sorority girls and the wandering hand, a lanky redhead passing in the other direction reached out and cupped him. He immediately became hard. The remainder of his trip to the bar was free of accosting, but he did find a few slips of paper with different girls' names and phone numbers in his pockets when he went for his wallet to pay for the beer.

He lifted the pitcher of green beer and mugs off the bar, held them over his head and began the trek back to his buddies at their table. Avoiding the tables along the wall this time, he crossed the middle of the room. All was fine until a guy had stepped on a girl's foot, and she jumped back and into Cole's path. The entire pitcher of green beer emptied over the petite blonde standing at Cole's left hip, soaking her.

She stood in shock partly because the beer was cold and partly because her wet blouse was now transparent. She felt like everyone in the bar was looking at her. All she could think at that moment was how glad she was that she had put on one of her good bras to go out that night.

From his vantage point, Cole looked down into the valley that was her cleavage. Rising gently from the pink lace bra that she wore he saw the swell of her generous breasts. Cole dropped the empty pitcher and mugs and immediately removed his T-shirt. He ignored the hoots and hollers from the crowd at the woman's revealing top and his striptease-like move, and covered the petite blonde with his shirt. Her friends quickly ushered her into the restroom. He watched the trio go into the women's room. She was the most beautiful woman he'd ever seen. It all happened too fast and like that she was gone, swept away. Jeff came over to where Cole still stood to check out what was going on with his friend.

"You okay?"

"Yes. No. Yes. I'm going to my car to get an extra shirt. Don't let her leave."

"Who?"

"The gorgeous blonde," Cole yelled over his shoulder to Jeff as he ran out of the pub.

Cole had an extra golf shirt with his clubs in the trunk

of his car. So he went out to the parking lot, retrieved the golf shirt and put it on. Eventually he began laughing to himself over the situation, but he did feel bad for the woman he had soaked, imagining her embarrassment at suddenly having so much of her body revealed in the crowded bar. She took his breath away. The small woman was quite beautiful. Cole was recalling the sight of her deep blue eyes, creamy skin and soft pink lips when his thoughts were disturbed by noise a few cars away in the parking lot. It was her, putting her wet shirt in her car. Cole immediately thought Jeff hadn't done as he'd asked him to. Luckily, Cole ran into her outside before she got away. The sight of this woman wearing his T-shirt sent Cole's thoughts racing.

"I am so sorry," Cole said as he walked over to her.

"It was accident. Don't worry about it." She held her hand out to Cole and introduced herself. "Sara Thompkins." Looking him up and down, she couldn't believe he was so incredibly drop dead gorgeous. She didn't know men this good looking really did exist.

"It's a pleasure to meet you," Cole said, and he meant it. He grasped the small hand that she offered. "Cole Becker." He looked into her eyes and felt he could see right into her soul. What he saw appeared to be a glow within her. He'd never experienced anything like that before and, frankly, it scared him. Her smile bore evidence of the warmth that filled her heart. Cole decided that he, from here on out, would make certain that no one ever extinguished her inner light. Her heart would never have the opportunity to grow cold.

"You're not leaving, are you, Sara?"

She hesitated before answering. "I was considering calling it a night." Gold flecks in his brown eyes shimmered in the reflection of the parking lot lights, mesmerizing her.

"Please don't leave. Come back inside. Please, Sara. I'll buy you a beer. I'll even let you carry it."

She giggled. "Seriously, thank you for the use of your shirt and your quick reaction. I had no idea how transparent that blouse became when it got wet!" Sara blushed and averted her gaze from Cole. She was a little embarrassed but also had found his eyes so mesmerizing it was hard for her to hold their gaze for any length of time.

Cole smiled. She was captivating. "I'm sorry that my technique in covering you with it was less than gentlemanly. I know that I grabbed a breast at one point. It was purely accidental, I assure you." It might have been an accident that time, but he wouldn't have minded being given the opportunity to go there again.

Sara bit her bottom lip to keep a laugh from escaping. She felt her cheeks warm and knew they were likely red. He probably was telling the truth, though she thought she wouldn't mind getting to know this man well enough that he'd decide to stake claim of her whole chest. No, no, her whole body.

"Oops." Cole tried to look as innocent as possible. "Let's go back in."

Cole's puppy dog eyes and pleading helped her make up her mind to stay.

He was glad she didn't object when he placed his hand on the small of her back and began to guide her back to the pub's entrance. Not only that she hadn't had a hissy fit, this woman was going back into the pub, not letting the incident ruin her evening. Cole really liked this woman already.

Sara and her entourage mingled with Cole and his friends on and off throughout the night.

"Man, Jeff gets one woman to dance with him and now he's got all the confidence in the world. He's danced with both of Sara's friends several times now." Bob's jealousy was evident.

"Maybe, but still Dan's the Man, Bob." Cole nodded in the direction of where Dan stood kissing Sara's friend, Denise. Cole laughed at how defeated Bob looked. "Aw, come on. You haven't exactly been sitting around alone all evening. I'm not buying your 'oh, woe is me' act."

Bob left Sara and Cole sitting at the table and headed toward the bar. They could hear him spouting foolish pick-up lines along the way. Sara and Cole turned to each other and laughed.

"Oh, Bob's a flirt. He'll have a girl on his arm in mere moments," Cole said.

"I'm going to check in with Denise, see if she thinks she'll need a ride home. Then I think I'm going to call it evening."

"I'll wait by the door to walk you to your car."

Sara returned without Denise, who'd decided she would get a ride home from Dan. After saying goodnight to the rest of her friends, Cole walked Sara to her car.

"Well, Cole, how may I return your shirt?" Sara looked down at Cole's T-shirt that she was wearing. It was several sizes too big for her.

"I'll be back in Greenville on Thursday. Care to meet me at the bistro downtown for dinner? You could return it to me then."

"Sure. How about seven o'clock?" Sara suggested.

"Perfect." He leaned in and kissed Sara ever so lightly on her lips. "Good night, Sara Thompkins," Cole whispered.

* * *

Cole grew up on his family's successful race horse farm with not much to worry about as far as creature comforts. Growing up he knew some kids in town didn't have it so good. But, like everyone else, he had his share of hardships. His mother died when he was twelve years old. Cole helped his dad, William, raise his younger brother and sister while he also helped to care for his elderly grandparents until they each passed away. After college Cole worked for his father doing marketing and managing contracts for the farm. His younger brother, James, was also employed by their father while he was in grad school working toward a master's degree in accounting.

He had the same experiences many children of wealthy families had when dating. It seemed the women he met were only after his money. So he learned to have one or two meetings for sex and to be sure the woman knew she had no future with him. Then he met Laurie and thought she was different. Her background hadn't bothered him. Laurie was the result of the rape her mother had endured when she was fifteen. He didn't see what that had to do with the person she was. But apparently not everyone, actually not many people at all, in Carnegie could see past the facts around her birth and allow themselves to get to know Laurie. She graduated high school a year after Cole. They never dated each other while they were in high school or while Cole was in college but ran across each other in Sully's Saloon in town about a year and a half ago. One dance led to another, and they started going out. She had been anxious when they first starting dating, often asking why he bothered to ask her out. He finally stopped trying to convince her that he wanted to be with her. Maybe Cole stuck with Laurie because it was convenient. Whatever it was, he eventually began to feel as though she was trying to manipulate him. He made sure Laurie was happy and feeling loved, but he realized she didn't really care as much for him. He wondered whether she even knew what he did working for his father. She never sacrificed her comfort or desires to do something Cole wanted if it didn't interest her. He began to think that dating Laurie was just something he did. Lately, it wasn't something he really wanted to do. He also realized at some point he began to notice other women more frequently.

He recalled one Sunday night in particular.
October 2009

It had become usual for Cole to pick Laurie up on Sunday nights and go into town to share a pizza at Mavis' Pizza Parlor. Mavis' place was the only pizza joint around for miles. Luckily she made great pizza. Normally, they would go there at around six o'clock. One Sunday afternoon, Cole went to the public athletic fields in town to watch his brother play polo. In high school Cole had played polo, and he felt he was a pretty good player back then, but his brother had always been better. James had a stockier, more athletic build than Cole, and probably a bit more drive to win than Cole did. The last time Cole played had been his senior year of high school, seven years prior. Going out on a Sunday to watch James play in a local men's league was important to the brothers, but it was also as involved as Cole got in polo after high school. Cole still rode his horse almost every day, and he preferred golf to polo. But Laurie didn't like watching polo. She never went to watch James play, not even just to spend time with her boyfriend.

Cole sat on the sidelines by himself that afternoon. Though some of their family members usually went to watch James play, he had been the only one to attend that day. He repositioned his large frame in the less-than-comfortable folding chair he was sitting in. He thought maybe he would stand up just to stretch out some. But then changed his mind when a twenty-something looking, tall blonde had set her folding chair not far from where Cole was sitting.

"Is this your cup?" she asked Cole.

Cole turned toward her delicate voice to see her holding out a plastic red cup. He didn't hear her question. She leaned toward him in her chair. The top she wore gapped in the front, allowing him a generous view of her chest. He reluctantly moved his gaze to her face. Large dark eyes were staring at him questioningly. "Well, is it? I don't want to just throw it away if it's your cup."

He looked at the cup in question. "Um, yes, it is my cup." Their fingers brushed against each other's when he grabbed the cup from her. The ensuing sparks he felt surprised him. "Thanks," he said with a smile and returned the cup to the cup holder in his folding chair.

"Do you know someone who's playing?" she asked.

"Yes, my brother. Number 3."

She pushed a length of her hair over her shoulder. "He's good. I've seen him play. I usually come to most games. My dad is number 2."

Dad? How old is this girl? Then a young guy placed a folding chair on the other side next to hers, sat and gave her a quick kiss. Cole heard him tell the girl he was sorry to have made her wait but had had a difficult time trying to find a parking spot.

Cole sat back in his chair. He considered making a move for this girl. That is, until she mentioned her dad was playing, and he realized she was younger than she looked. Her boyfriend showing up kind of kept him from making a move as well. Thoughts of Laurie never came across his mind through it all. However, it was the first sign that made Cole aware he was looking for more than what he was getting from his relationship with Laurie.

Well, he thought, *at least I got a decent view of some*

cleavage out of the whole exchange.

Following the match, Cole helped load up James' horse while James showered and changed in the clubhouse. He heard James' voice and some laughing as Cole closed the trailer doors. One of James' teammates had his arm around his brother's shoulders and they were both laughing. Cole climbed into the driver's side of the farm's large pick-up truck and waited for his brother. A few minutes later, James threw his bag of gear into the bed of the truck and settled into the passenger seat beside Cole. It was a deal the brothers had made a long time ago, if Cole was in the truck after one of James' polo matches, the gear bag was not allowed in the truck cab with them. Cole was certain the stench violated some basic human right.

The polo field was in the middle of their small hometown not far away from their family's farm. Cole drove slowly up the farm's long dirt driveway and parked in front of the barn. Once James' horse was taken care of and in its stall for the evening, Cole drove the truck and trailer to park it with the other farm vehicles. As he climbed out of the truck he asked James, "Wanna head to Sully's for some beers?" referring to the local watering hole. Cole read James' questioning look and explained, "Laurie texted a bit ago, she said she wasn't feeling well and cancelled on me for tonight." Serious and intense almost to a fault, Cole was slightly surprised at his younger brother's response.

"Shit yeah!" James whooped.

Cole traced a path through the sweat on his beer bottle as he sat by himself at a table. He eyed James across the room talking to a ranch hand who worked at the Miller's cattle ranch nearby. Cole couldn't remember the guy's name. The door to the pub opened and three guys walked in. One was Tanner Ford, Bridgeton Pass' foreman. He saw Cole and headed to his table.

"Mind if I join ya?" Tanner asked. He was a middle-aged guy, tall and still in good shape from not being afraid to continue to work hard on the Becker's' farm over the years. He looked similar to his cousin, J.P. Ryan, Bridgeton Pass's horse trainer and Cole's sister's main squeeze—only squeeze.

"Not at all." Cole sat up straighter in his chair.

"Slow night in here tonight," Tanner observed, then asked for a beer when a waitress came by their table.

Cole ordered another beer, then commented to Tanner, "Sure is. I came with James after his polo match earlier." He figured he should head off the expected question and told Tanner that Laurie had cancelled their usual Sunday evening date for pizza.

Tanner looked over at James where he had been talking with some other guys across the room, then back at Cole.

"And you've just been sitting here all evening?"

"Pretty much, I was contemplating heading back home. Nothing much happening here." Then he added, "You know, there just aren't any available single women in Carnegie anymore. Seems they've all gotten married or moved away for college and never came back."

Tanner didn't point out that Cole was in a relationship already. Rather, he smiled at Cole, letting him know he understood about the lack of women in town. He had a good ten years on Cole and had been coming to Sully's Saloon to drink for about just as long. He knew what it was like to look for love living in a small town. But Tanner was feeling old. He wasn't looking for love anymore.

"Any luck finding any new decent prospects for the farm?" The waitress had delivered their beers. Tanner was referring to prospects for purchasing a horse that could likely become a champion race horse. Bridgeton Pass

Farms hadn't had a winning champion in their stables for some time now. Not for lack of trying. They were in a slump and knew that financially it would eventually begin to hurt.

"Got a few foals we're interested in. We'll be checking them out."

Tanner nodded.

Now, if only I could just find a few new lady interests for myself to check out. He tried to ask himself why he was thinking like this. He and Laurie had been together for a while. He thought they had been happy together. He decided it wasn't worth thinking about. He wanted more. Cole threw back the rest of his beer, then told Tanner he was calling it a night and heading home.

Thereafter, not really having any desire to analyze his relationship with Laurie any further, Cole pretty much went on with life as it had been which, if he had thought about it, was pretty sad for a single twenty-three-year-old college educated professional. Life for Cole, working for his father doing the marketing and managing contracts for the farm, had meant he made occasional trips into Greenville for business. The upside was the rounds of golf that he managed to fit in between all the meetings.

He said, she said.
Several weeks later

It was during one of his occasional games of golf with Jeff when Cole got the spark he needed to at least start thinking about making some kind of change in his life.

Jeff's cousin, Angela, was a friend of one of Laurie's co-workers. As Cole placed his ball and tee, Jeff told Cole he heard something recently which Cole might find interesting.

"My cousin asked me last week if it was true that you were planning to pop the question with Laurie."

"What?" Cole asked incredulously and stepped back from the tee.

"Apparently, Laurie's expecting it and talking to her co-workers about it."

"Great," Cole said under his breath. "I've no such plan, Jeff. I don't know where she got the idea from."

"Hey, no worries if you do or don't. Just thought you'd want to know what she's saying if it wasn't true."

"Thanks." Cole turned to the ball he had set on the tee and lined up the club for his drive.

That feeling that Cole was being manipulated came over him anew. He had to find out if what Jeff heard was true. Cole would not allow a woman to think he could be manipulated, for whatever reason.

Slim pickins.
Late October 2009

Cole was standing outside the arena fence, talking to J.P. Ryan. An apprentice at Bridgeton Pass, J.P. worked under the guidance of the farm's long-time horse trainer, Manuel Rodriguez. Apparently waiting for the dust to settle, Manuel waited before making his way across the arena to where J.P. stood with the horse they were working with. He saw no sense in walking through the dust and breathing it in. Manuel was feeling his age lately and as such was making concessions for himself more readily.

Manuel crossed the arena and reached J.P. as the man talked over the arena fence to Cole.

"Buenos días, Cole."

"Buenos días, Manuel. I was just asking J.P. how he felt about our current stock of horses."

21

"Not too bueno. Some have potential but will need more work." It was evident to Manuel that he knew this was not what Cole had wanted to hear. "There is an auction at the beginning of the year which may present us with some options." He was trying to sound hopeful.

"Yeah." Cole had lost interest and his attention wandered. "Looks like selling one off might be the best option for now. We'll have to discuss which horse it should be."

At the sound of Cole's sixteen-year-old sister, Audra, climbing to sit on the fence at the other side of the arena they all turned to look. Cole's little sister liked to watch Manuel and J.P. working with the horses. In reality, she was infatuated with and liked to watch J.P.

"Ella es el amor golpeó," Manuel said with a grin.

"What did he say?" J.P. whispered to Cole.

Cole's understanding of Spanish was limited, but he had been pretty certain Manuel had said that Audra was love struck. Not wanting to inflate J.P.'s ego by even loosely translating Manuel's observation of Audra's admiration for J.P., he said, "He likes the way this horse gallops."

A snicker escaped Manuel over Cole's cleverly altered translation.

With few prospective horses of interest to the farm, Cole wondered if Laurie still planned to marry into the Becker family when Bridgeton Pass' future was not so bright. She never showed much interest in the farm. Likely, Cole thought, she did not have any idea about the slump. So when she began asking questions after what Jeff told Cole, he couldn't help but wonder if someone had questioned Laurie about the wisdom of her plan. At first he thought maybe she was gathering information only to try and find out just how bad off the farm was. Maybe she just wondered if what she had heard were merely rumors.

Power lunch.
November 2009

Usually Cole enjoyed the chicken salad sandwiches from the diner in town. But as Laurie fired questions at him all through their lunch together he couldn't get himself to eat the sandwich. It had begun to taste like sawdust. Her questions centered around Bridgeton Pass' chances for the next race season.

"I'm finding our lunch conversation today interesting, Laurie. You've never shown much interest in my work."

Her expression fell, proving the smile she was wearing had only been pasted on to feign interest.

"Well, uh, I hear that the new trainer is pretty good."

"And that piqued your interest?'

"Of course." Then she added with a sigh of frustration and a whining tone to her voice, "I'm trying to take more of an interest, Cole. You always seem to want me to take more of an interest in what you do."

"Yes, well, genuine interest would be appreciated. But Laurie, you saying that you want to take an interest is quite different. Please, don't pretend for my benefit."

"I'm not pretending, Cole. I am interested in how well the farm does."

Cole had thought her choice of wording just then had been more accurate in terms of where her interests had been lying.

"Exactly, Laurie. Your interest is in the farm's success, not in me." He was finished with his lunch. Cole waived to the waitress for their check.

"Cole, please. You're twisting my words. I care about you. I'm trying to show that."

He looked briefly at Laurie but saw little sincerity.

"Check, please, Suellen."

Benefit Dinner with benefits.
December 2009

The Saturday before Christmas that year Cole attended a dinner with his father and James to benefit a charity which the Becker family supported for generations. It was a formal affair and promised to be a somewhat boring evening. Dressed in tuxedos, they would mingle during the cocktail hour, take their assigned seats at well-dressed tables and listen to key speakers tell of their contributions to the charity as well as why everyone should donate like them. The Becker businessmen had attended the annual holiday benefit dinner for many years. In addition, they attended the occasional less formal benefit dinners held throughout the year. It was an opportunity for the Beckers to show their support as a family and as a business in the community. For James these benefit dinners, like any social event, were a setting in which to bag an easy score. William had recently felt the need to have a discussion about this behavior with James. Cole knew this because James told Cole about the ridiculous talk their father felt he needed to have with James. Laurie constantly turned down Cole's invitation to formal events, claiming they made her uncomfortable. No matter how Cole tried to convince Laurie that she had no reason to feel that way she always refused to attend, so Cole stopped asking her to join him some time ago.

They barely arrived when James abandoned Cole and his father to become acquainted with an event staff server. Cole smirked as he watched James introduce himself to the woman. Turning to his father, Cole found that his father left his side as well. William was talking with a group of gentlemen. Cole figured he might as well try to enjoy the evening and that's why he didn't think twice about Laurie while he approached a tall brunette who caught his eye. Or when he took her into a supply closet and lifted her skirt.

On the Sunday evening following the benefit dinner, Cole thought he may have felt a small amount of guilt when he sat with Laurie eating pizza at Mavis' Pizza Parlor. He and Laurie never talked specifically about them being exclusive. He didn't think she had been with anyone else since they had begun dating. And as he sat thinking about it, he wasn't sure that he would have minded if she had. Their relationship had stalled, Cole thought. All the while, Laurie had been saying how she resented that Cole chose to go riding with his sister last Saturday rather than to spend the afternoon with her. He tried to explain that he already made the plans with his sister before Laurie asked him to spend Saturday with her. She didn't understand why he didn't reschedule his plans with his sister, especially since he was going to be at his brother's polo match all afternoon the next day. Eventually he just stopped listening to her. When Laurie sensed this, she asked, "What's wrong?"

"Nothing."

"You're not listening. Are you okay?"

Laurie wasn't a raving beauty, but Cole had liked her long, silky brown hair. Her eyes were set too close together and her lips were thin. He had never enjoyed kissing Laurie all that much. There had been no...substance.

I'm bored. "I'm fine." His smile was forced.

A dollop of pizza sauce dripped from the slice she had been holding and landed in her lap. She tossed the slice back onto the pizza pan in the middle of their table and held her hands up, looking at the sauce staining her jeans.

"Oh, fiddlesticks."

Fiddlesticks? Who says fiddlesticks? "I'll get you a wet cloth."

Cole went to the counter and asked Mavis for a wet cloth. As he explained why he needed it Dillon Chambray joined him at the counter.

"Hey, Dillon. Nice to see you," Cole greeted the business colleague. "I didn't see you at the benefit dinner last weekend."

"I was there," Dillon said. He had cocked his head sideways as he looked at Cole questioningly. "You must not have noticed," he lowered his voice, "you were busy in the supply closet."

Cole's gaze moved from Dillon to Laurie, who was staring at him with a hurt look. "Nice, Dillon. Thanks, buddy." He grabbed the wet cloth Mavis had left for him on the counter and returned to the table with Laurie. When he tried to help by wiping at the sauce on Laurie's lap, she pushed his hands away.

"Stop, Cole. Don't touch me." Her tone was sharp. She took the cloth from him and cleaned the spot. "Take me home," she demanded.

The windshield wipers moved slowly, clearing away the rain as he drove Laurie home. "About Dillon's comment," he started.

"I don't want to talk about it."

"Why? It obviously upset you."

When she didn't respond, he glanced at her. Her head was turned away from him, looking out her side window. He hated when she wouldn't talk to him. How could they work through any problems if she didn't talk about what was bothering her?

"Laurie, we've never made any commitment to each other. Never said that either of us couldn't date other people."

"No, we just haven't dated other people." She lowered

her voice. "Or fucked them in a closet."

"Oh, tell me you haven't been with anyone else since we started going out."

"No! I can't believe you even asked me that. Why would I? We had a sort of unstated understanding that we were together."

"You mean that you assumed we did, Laurie."

"How many other women have you slept with, Cole? Oh my God. Don't answer that."

He hadn't been with anyone else until the evening of the benefit dinner, but he wasn't going to tell that to Laurie. It would have made it appear as though he felt more for her than he did. At one point he had thought maybe he did feel deeply for her, but then he knew that wasn't true. Their relationship was over. He didn't see the point in letting her believe they could continue even with mutual consent to date other people. But he had to be sure Laurie understood this.

"Laurie, we don't care enough for each other to continue seeing each other." He had pulled his truck into her driveway and put it into park.

"Is that how you feel? When did you start feeling that way? Were you going to tell me? Or were you just going to find other women and keep me on the side? You know no one else will go out with me, Cole."

That was enough. He wasn't going to allow her to try to guilt him into staying with her because of her past.

"Stop it, Laurie. Stop trying to hide behind your past. And that has nothing to do with why I will or will not go out with you. I'm tired of that conversation, so let it go." He could see the tears welling in her eyes but it didn't stop him from saying, "Let me go."

"Fine." She opened the door and stepped out without a goodbye.

Cole drove directly home after dropping Laurie off.

One night stands, a few dates, one closet fuck and this relationship, Cole contemplated his history with women as he drove. Nothing fulfilling, he had decided. He just wasn't a player. James, now he was a player. Cole laughed out loud. His stoic brother was harmless, just very active in his sex life. No, Cole wasn't a player. He was almost surprised when he, as he thought about it, realized what he wanted was to meet his true love. It shouldn't have surprised him, really. His parents had found true love in each other, he was sure of that. They had a deeply passionate, loving relationship. He could see that he wanted much of what his father had in his relationship with his wife. Cole remembered his father saying that no woman was more beautiful, inside and out, than Cole's mother, Maddie. His father would stare at his mother with what Cole now knew was a smoldering look of desire. When Cole was a kid he had just thought his father looked goofy at his mother. His father had taken care of their mother, loved and protected her while she was healthy in their marriage and all through her illness to her death. Cole knew that when he met the woman who was meant for him, he would know. He would want nothing but to be with her, love and protect her. Much like his father had done for his mother. He longed for that kind of relationship. He just hadn't realized that was what he wanted until now.

Cole arrived home, parked his car and went to the media room in the main house. More comfortable than the formal living room on the main floor of the house, the media room had recliners and couches, an in-home theater, a pool table, a wet bar, and a refrigerator. There was a hockey game on, and Cole assumed James would be there watching it.

"I figured you'd be here."

"And you were correct."

Cole grabbed a beer from the fridge and fell into one of the recliners in front of the flat screen television.

"Did you enjoy pizza night with Laurie?"

"We broke up."

James sat up in his recliner. "You don't say?"

"Yup. All done. On to greener pastures."

"You don't seem too broken about it."

"It was inevitable. The relationship grew stale. Besides, she started getting all weird about how the farm is doing and that kind of shit. She never cared before. She's never even cared about what I do for the farm."

"Mmm. Never thought Laurie would become a gold digger. Just never know." James' gaze was on the television. He took a swig of his beer. "Yeah, score!"

The brothers high-fived each other.

"Yeah. Don't need that kind of crap in my life." Cole returned to their conversation.

"You looked like you needed that brunette in the closet the other night at the benefit dinner."

"Shit. You saw that too? Did the whole place see us go into the closet? I thought we were pretty slick about it."

"I don't know who else saw you, but they were probably the only other person who did 'cause, yeah, you guys weren't obvious about it. She was hot." James wiggled his eyebrows at his brother.

"She was." Cole had a satisfied look on his face.

"Thong?"

"Nothing."

"Commando?"

"Bare bottom is right."

"Wow. I didn't get that lucky."

"What did you get? I saw you pounce on the server as soon as we walked through the door."

"Not her, but her friend. Another server. She brought her bottle opener with her and met me in a bathroom."

"Her bottle opener?" Cole rolled his eyes at his brother. He didn't know his brother to be big on socializing and parties. James only had a few stale friends that Cole knew of. All of them intellectuals, quiet, and intense. He did know James liked sex. No strings, no relationship just sex. He also knew James liked toys but some of them he wasn't sure of. He didn't really want to know what his brother did with them.

"She was okay." The guys drifted from their conversation to focusing on the hockey game as the competition had become more intense.

That was when Cole began to start waiting for the hurt. But it never came, and he was surprised at how little he missed Laurie. And then he met Sara.

About your T-shirt...
March 2010

Cole met Sara at the bistro as planned the week after he met her on St. Patty's Day. Cole suggested the bistro because it was his favorite place in Greenville to eat. They had a really good chef, an exceptional wine list, and excellent service. He requested a table in front of the glass wall overlooking the bistro's own herb and vegetable gardens. He enjoyed their evening. Being with Sara, he decided, was comfortable. There were no awkward prolonged moments of silence. In fact, they laughed a lot. Interestingly, Sara claimed at the beginning of their evening that she forgot the T-shirt Cole had lent to her at the pub, the reason for their meeting at the bistro that evening. Later in the evening, after some wine had loosened her tongue, Sara admitted that she purposefully hadn't brought the T-shirt to return.

"I have to confess something, Cole."

"Oh."

"I didn't forget your T-shirt."

"You didn't."

"No. I've been sleeping with it." Sara looked at Cole to see his reaction. He shifted in his seat and leaned forward as if to encourage her to go on. His eyes were large and dark, staring directly at her. He looked as though he would be on her in a second had she let him know that was what she wanted.

"I'm sorry, Cole, but I don't want to give it back. It smells like you and reminds me of the night we met." She hoped he wouldn't ask her for it back.

"I'll make a deal with you."

"And what would that be?"

"I'll let you keep it if agree to go on another date with me."

"That's easy. It's a deal."

Her kisses at the end of their evening together proved to be as delicious as he hoped and let him know she planned to see him again. But the fact that Sara drove her own car to meet him at the bistro let him know she didn't plan on more than dinner with him that night. He wasn't surprised when she didn't invite him back to her place. He was surprised to realize that it actually didn't bother him as much as it may have in the past. Many of the dates Cole went on while he was in high school and college, before Laurie, were one night stands or short-lived relationships. His year and a half relationship with Laurie started once he was out of college and was the only real relationship that he had had. Now if Sara had invited him back to her place he wouldn't have said 'no' but as he left her in Greenville and drove the half hour home he thought about how his evening with this woman whose every nuance made him unable to think straight had ended. Everything from her heated gazes to the silky blouse that subtly bared her cleavage and even allowed him peeks at a nipple through her sheer bra beneath let him know she wanted him. Before getting into her car and driving away she left him with a sensual kiss that sealed for him her undoubted interest and a look that begged his understanding when she told him good night.

Nothing about the way that evening ended made him feel that he wouldn't see her again. So Cole decided he was okay with the idea of first getting to know Sara better. It wasn't his usual way with women in the past, but he felt that when he did take her to bed he didn't plan on it being some quick and dirty one night stand.

The food ain't that good.
Late March 2010

Cole had called Sara in the evening, the day after their first dinner together.

"I take it that you made it back to your apartment okay?"

"I did. And, Cole, I had a really great time with you. I'm glad you called me because I meant it when I agreed to go on another date with you."

"Great. I couldn't help but call you right away to make plans." He didn't see the point in waiting some requisite amount of time before calling Sara again. If he scared her off, so be it.

"I like that you did. You seem to follow your heart and not some set of socially drawn rules. We didn't talk about it last night but, and I know this may sound ironic, it was because I like you that I didn't bring you home with me."

Cole laughed. "I get it, Sara. I'm flattered actually now that you say that. I can't say that I wouldn't have gone with you'd you asked. In the end, I'm glad we're getting to know each other outside the bedroom first. I can tell there's more to you than a pretty face, gorgeous figure, heavenly eyes..."

"Stop!" They both laughed.

"It's true." He changed the subject for her sake. "Listen, when can I see you again?"

And so, as they had planned that evening, Sara drove to Carnegie on a weeknight for their second date a week later. They met at the diner in town. Cole told Sara to dress casual as there were no fancy restaurants in his small hometown.

When she walked into the diner that evening in her tight jeans, snug T-shirt and worn cowboy boots he thought she looked awfully hot. They laughed when they had looked at each other and had seen that they were wearing basically the same thing.

"This is small town casual attire."

"It sure is," Cole had agreed. He admired the curve of her breasts that the white T-shirt she wore strained to accommodate.

After they placed their food order, Sara let Cole know that she would need to leave soon after they finished dinner since she had to get up early for work the next day. Then she asked, "do you like having to travel into Greenville so often for work?'

"I'm only out there one or two times every month or so and only occasionally for an overnight. It's not bad. Do you travel for work ever?"

"As a matter of fact, I'm going to be leaving for two weeks in St. Louis in a few days. I'll be doing some training on a new product."

Cole slid from his seat in the booth and went around the table to sit next to Sara on her side of the booth. He leaned in close with his arm behind her shoulders across the back of the seat. "Since you'll be leaving me early tonight and be gone for two weeks, I want to be right up close to you while I've got you." He placed several soft kisses along her neck.

"All right, love birds." The waitress, Suellen, drawled a warning of her impending approach for them before placing their plates on the table. Cole heard the waitress say "Enjoy," then she muttered something else he couldn't hear as she walked away.

Cole turned back to Sara with a smile and a small laugh. He laid his hand on her thigh under the table, and as their meal progressed so did his hand up her thigh. He watched her face as he turned in his seat for a better angle. She slid her legs apart just enough for Cole to fit his fingers between them. Her eyes searched his face. "Here?" she asked, looking around the diner nervously.

"Here," he said simply, then began to rub at the seam of her jeans. They continued to hold each other's gaze. Cole's neutral expression gave nothing away. Sara licked her lips and leaned into the sweet pressure that his fingers were eliciting at her core. She began to roll her hips and closed her eyes as the pleasant sensations began to mount. He felt her heat, and Cole imaged the wetness he knew was there beneath the layers under the ends of his fingers. He leaned his head closer to her. She felt the tips of her hardened nipples lightly brush over his chest through their clothes.

"Look at me, Sara. Open your eyes. Look at me." Her breaths became uneven. With his lips just grazing her ear, he whispered, "You're beautiful." He barely heard his name escape her mouth. And when she needed to bite her bottom lip to keep from crying out as she came, he covered her mouth with his. His kiss was hungry at first and slowed as he felt her body relaxing.

"Dag nabbit, you two, here's your check." Suellen left

the slip on the table. Cole heard her mumble as she walked away, "Never knew the food here to be that good."

Cole broke their kiss and leaned his forehead on hers. They smiled at each other.

He pulled out his wallet and threw a couple of bills onto the table. "Come on, let's go. You've got to get home." Cole held his hand out to help Sara from the booth and began to walk away, holding her hand. Sara stopped abruptly and looked back at the booth.

"What's wrong?" Cole asked.

"Nothing, that booth will always be my favorite," Sara teased. She leaned close and whispered, "You fuckin' blew my mind there."

Cole smiled. "Yeah, I did, didn't I?"

He held her car door open for her when they reached it in the diner's parking lot.

"Can I make you dinner at my place when I get back from St. Louis?"

"I'd love that. Can I bring my pajamas?"

"If that's what you sleep in, sure." She laughed, imaging him in a matching set ready for bed.

"Actually, I sleep naked." He stole a quick kiss and then became serious. "I want you, Sara."

"When I get back you can have me." She had a look of promise in her eyes. But when she licked her lips, he covered her mouth with his. His kiss was hard, hungry, and impatient. He emitted a sound something like a growl, then released her.

"Hurry back," he said and closed her car door once she slipped into the driver's seat. He still felt that they made the right decision to get to know each other before he bedded her, but he wasn't a saint, and he was growing impatient with his need for her.

And that was when his mother-in-law had come into the picture.

Dinner at Sara's.
April 2010

Cole took the steps into Sara's brick apartment building two at a time the evening that he went there for dinner. She was back from her business trip to St. Louis, and he could hardly wait to see her again.

He took in the sight of her when she opened the door to welcome him in. Her blue eyes made him melt right there at her door.

"Hello, Sara." He pulled her close, molding her body to his and took the kiss he couldn't wait any longer for. She put her arms around his neck and returned his kiss with as much desire as he had shown her. He released his grip from around her tiny waist and closed her apartment door.

"Well, hello to you too." She was breathless when his lips left hers. She took the bottle of wine that he held out to her and thanked him for it. "Dinner is just about ready. Please, have seat in the living room."

She disappeared into the apartment's small kitchen. Cole took in the modern feel of the apartment. The walls were painted cool blue and gray colors. Her furniture was primarily made from white leather and metal. The artwork was stark and crisp but provided the color in the rooms, primarily orange, red, and greens. He took a seat on the couch, and Sara returned a moment later with the open wine bottle and two wine glasses. She set the glasses on the coffee table in front of where he was sitting, then sat next to him. She kicked her flats off of her feet and pulled one leg under her. Sitting like this, her knee was leaning on his thigh. Cole liked how obviously comfortable she was around him already. He poured wine for each of them.

Sara picked up the bottle and inspected the label. He had chosen to bring a pinot noir of very good vintage which had been, therefore, moderately high priced. Appropriate for just drinking and with dinner but not over-the-top.

"Nice wine, Cole. Thank you very much for sharing this."

He wondered whether she knew wine or was just being polite. It didn't matter either way to him, but thought it would be nice if she really did have some knowledge about wine.

"So, this is where my T-shirt now lives," he joked, looking around the apartment from his seat on the couch.

Sara blushed and laughed. "Thanks for letting me keep it."

"I'm flattered. But I was more flattered that you agreed to see me again."

"I hope I wasn't being too forward in asking you to have dinner at my apartment."

"I hope I don't sound too arrogant in saying that I assume it's not your style to lure just any guy to your place."

"You don't and it's not. I just want to have you all to myself tonight."

Cole's eyes darkened. "Be careful or we'll never eat this wonderful meal you've made."

A bright smile came over her face. "Come on, let's eat!" She popped up from the couch, grabbed the bottle and her glass of wine, leaving her shoes, and went into the kitchen with Cole following her.

The meal was utterly delicious. Sara had wanted to be a chef but opted for a more stable career in computers, she told Cole that evening. She fulfilled her yearning to cook by volunteering at a local soup kitchen. Cole doubted it was as fulfilling as the artistry of being a chef would have been for her.

"But cooking for a large amount of people is not the same as being a chef."

"No, but cooking for the soup kitchen fulfills other things about cooking for me, like making something that is better than 'good enough' from barely no offerings."

He wondered if the recipients appreciated her efforts but thought she would have probably done the job no matter if they did or not. Eventually, he realized he had been holding her fingers lightly in his palm, stroking his thumb across the back of her hand as he listened to her. Through the candles in the middle of the table, he admired her soft features and striking blue eyes. But it was that Sara asked if he liked his job, especially because he worked with immediate family, that appealed to him, probably as much as her obvious physical beauty.

When the meal was finished, Cole helped clear the dishes from the table.

"I'm sorry, I like to cook but not baking. Desserts are not my thing. I do have some ice cream in the freezer if you want to satisfy your sweet tooth."

Cole was leaning against the kitchen counter with one ankle crossed over the other and his arms folded across his chest. He was sex incarnate wearing a lightweight camel sweater that brought out the gold flecks in his brown eyes, dark blue jeans that fit perfectly and butter-soft leather driving shoes, no socks.

"I don't have much of a sweet tooth. Not for desserts at least."

With a hungry stare and sultry movement, Sara walked toward Cole from across the room. She dropped her eyes as she moved past him, then picked up his gaze again from over her shoulder as she walked toward the bedroom. The potency of her eroticism hung in the air. He unfolded his arms, uncrossed his ankles, pushed off the counter with his hip, and followed her into the bedroom.

Her top lay on the floor at her feet, and she had shimmied out of her capri pants. He sat in the chair in the corner of her room to watch her finish undressing. Sara looked at him sitting relaxed in her reading chair with one ankle crossed over his other knee, his eyes heavily hooded and wearing a grin.

"Aren't you going to play also?" she asked.

"Keep going. I'll join you in a minute."

A sexy smile crept across her face. She reached back, unhooked her bra and let it fall. Leaning forward she hooked her thumbs in the strings of her bikini underwear and pushed them down to step out of them. She pulled the sheets on her bed back.

"Wait," Cole said and let his eyes move over her body completely. He stood and took the few steps across her room to her. He hadn't imagined that she'd be as gorgeous as she was and her body took his breath away. With one finger he lifted her chin to look into her eyes.

"You are absolutely the most beautiful woman I've ever met." He reached around with his hand on her lower back and pulled her to him. With his other hand he cupped the back of her head to bring her mouth to his. They kissed, tasting each other and exploring. Neither had been anywhere near finished with the kiss when Sara's phone rang. She let it ring a few times, but she had to answer it.

"I'm so sorry, Cole, but I have to answer it, my mother is very sick. It could be about her." She sat naked on the edge of her bed, cradling the phone to her ear.

"Hello. Oh. Okay. Yes. Right. Okay. Thanks. See you soon." She let out a sigh as she slowly returned the phone to its charger.

When she turned to face him, Cole was holding out her bra, shirt, capris, and panties for her.

"Anything I can do?"

She shook her head that there was not. She took the

clothes that Cole held out for her and began to dress.

"That was my sister, Beth. Mom fell. She was just taken to the hospital by ambulance."

"I could go with you if you'd like." He knew they had just met, so he left it up to her whether she wanted his support. Whatever she was comfortable with would be okay with him.

"That's a kind offer, Cole, but we live on a farm out past Columbia. My mom's being taken to a hospital in Columbia."

It was about an hour and a half drive from Sara's apartment in Greenville to Columbia. Cole knew Sara's car was older, it was ten o'clock at night, and she had drunk some wine. Being as petite as she was, he wasn't sure how alcohol affected her.

"I'd feel better if I drove you in my car."

"It's too far, Cole. You hardly know me. It's too much to ask, but I do appreciate the offer."

"Sara, I'd probably feel the same way if I were you. But look at it from where I'm standing right now. You'd be driving a long distance alone late at night in an older car. You're anxious and worried about your mother and you've had some wine. I couldn't live with myself if anything happened to you tonight. I'll get you to the hospital, then I'll set up in hotel for the night. We'll take it from there depending on what we find out when we get there. Please let me do this."

Sara's car was old and when she thought about the situation as he had put it to her, she knew she would have felt the same sense of responsibility if she had been in his shoes. "Okay. Thanks, Cole."

After the fall.
April 2010

Cole let Sara out at the hospital's emergency room doors, then went to park his car. In the waiting room he found Sara talking to a woman and a man who looked to be a few years older than Sara. She introduced them to Cole as her sister, Beth, and Beth's husband, Ricky. Her sister explained that their mother broke her hip and was in surgery. Beth and Ricky had been on their way back to the surgical waiting area when Sara arrived. Cole left Sara to be with her family, but not before he gave her what he had hoped was a comforting hug and kiss on her temple.

"I'm going to get a room at the hotel just down the street from the hospital. Call me if you need anything tonight, a ride, a toothbrush, another hug. Okay?"

She nodded in agreement.

"Please, feel free to call me, for anything."

She rose up onto her tiptoes and kissed him softly. "Thank you," she whispered.

Though the hotel suite was comfortable and nicely appointed, Cole couldn't sleep. He called James and filled him in on where he was and what was going on. He watched late night television, parts of two different old movies and took a shower. By two o'clock he thought Sara's mother had to be out of surgery. He hoped her mother had done well through surgery. Sara said her mother was sick before the fall, and Cole wondered if her illness could keep her from healing well. Cole then began to wonder if Sara's sister took Sara back to their family farm to sleep. He wouldn't have minded if Sara called to have him pick her up at the hospital and bring her back to his hotel room. In fact, he hoped she would be in his bed that night but didn't want to take advantage of her at a time like that.

It irritated him that their evening ended so abruptly. And Cole had more than a taste of what the night could have been like, before it ended. In the dark of his hotel room he lay thinking of Sara standing before him earlier that evening, naked. Her skin looked like porcelain. What little amount of her skin he did have the opportunity to touch was simply wonderful to feel. His body reacted to the memory, tenting his boxers. He wondered just how big of a jerk he was for the resentment he felt toward her mother for having taken away his opportunity to be deep inside Sara that evening. But he wasn't going to dwell on those kinds of dark thoughts. He wanted another opportunity with her and soon. He wanted to feel more of her, all of her. He was driving himself crazy. His thoughts of her consumed him. So he took a cold shower.

A soft knock on the door of his hotel suite took him from his thoughts. *Damn, not only was my opportunity with her disrupted, but I can't even get the opportunity to think about her without getting disturbed.* But just then he figured it had to be her at the door. He'd rather have had the real thing than just his memory of her. He turned on the light and let her into his room. She dropped her bag and turned the lights off, then wrapped her arms around his waist. He could tell she was utterly exhausted. He gave her a firm hug, then scooped her into his arms to put her onto the bed.

"Cole, I…"

"Shhh…" He removed her shoes, capris, and her blouse, leaving her underwear on, then covered her with the sheet and blanket. He sat on the edge of the bed next to her and pushed a piece of her hair away from her eyes. "How is your mother?"

"She's sleeping. The surgery to repair her broken hip went okay. Beth and Ricky went home. They have a house on the far side of our farm's property. They also have a young daughter. I would have had to sleep on the floor at their house and I didn't want to stay in the big farmhouse by myself, so I had them drop me off here."

"Good. Can I get you anything? Are you hungry?"

"No, thanks. But thanks for letting me stay here." He stroked her hair and saw her eyes starting to close.

"I'm going to sleep in the other room. The couch pulls out to a bed."

"I'm sorry about tonight."

"Don't worry. I want you, Sara, but tonight couldn't be the night. You're exhausted. Get some sleep."

She nodded and closed her eyes. Cole kissed her forehead and then her lips. "Good night, Sara Thompkins."

Sara knew she probably should have gone to her family's farmhouse and stayed there. It was silly, but she wanted to be in the hotel room with Cole. She couldn't sleep with him. There was too much going on, too much worry and unanswered questions. She wanted their first time to be special, like it would have been that night. Not in a hotel room when she was a messy ball of stress. But she liked knowing Cole was near, just in the next room, while she slept. She really didn't want to be alone.

Cole sat in his boxers on the couch in the hotel suite that night, knowing there was no way he was going to sleep. He felt sorry that Sara had to feel his excitement as she hugged him at the door when all she wanted to do was sleep, but there wasn't much he could have done about it. And then she was half naked in the bed he had just been in, merely steps away in the next room. It was going to be a long night.

Sara waited until Cole closed the door to the suite's bedroom, smiling just thinking of Cole's kindness. She appreciated him letting her crash in his hotel room, and the care he took to undress her and ask if she needed anything. She guessed that she couldn't blame a guy for not realizing that sleeping in an underwire bra was not comfortable. She slipped it off under the covers, got out of bed and found her bag on the floor by the bed in the dark. She pulled out her nightshirt, Cole's T-shirt that he lent her on St. Patty's Day, and slipped it on. She let the familiar comfort of the worn shirt and his scent that lingered on it lull her to sleep.

The sounds of someone moving about behind the closed door of the suite's bedroom roused Cole the next morning. The amount of sleep he got was limited, he was exhausted. Still, he woke with morning wood. Geez, he had it bad. The poor woman was worried about her sick, elderly mother, and all he could think about was hopping into bed with her. Coffee, he needed coffee so he could try and think straight. Did Sara drink coffee? Probably. He stood from the couch and padded softly across the suite's living room to knock on the bedroom door.

"Come in." Her voice was like a sheet of silk flowing over him.

He opened the door and looked around the room for her. He found her standing over her bag, pulling clothes out of it and wearing his T-shirt. The sight of her looking sleepy with mussed hair and the pebble of her hard nipples evident under his T-shirt invited desires he worked hard to tamp down. Why did he come to her bedroom? Oh, yes.

"Coffee?"

"Yes, please." She didn't look at him. If she did, he would have pounced from across the room at her. Just as he was leaving and closing the bedroom door, she called his name.

"I'm going to shower quickly and go to the hospital." She dropped the pair of jeans that she had been holding onto the bed and looked at him. "I'll be at the hospital hanging around my mother's bed all day. You may as well head back home. I'll have my sister drive me back to Greenville once my mom is settled."

"Are you sure? I don't mind staying and taking you back."

"I appreciate that, but I don't know how long it will be before she is settled. I'm sure she's going to need help at home for a bit at least."

It was a reasonable plan.

"Let me order that coffee and a muffin so you can at least have that before you go to the hospital." Cole gave her a weak smile and closed the door behind him. He heard the shower turn on as he ordered room service.

May 2010

Two weeks after Cole left Sara with a kiss in front of the hospital in Columbia he still hadn't heard from her. He didn't call her because he didn't want to add to the stress that she was dealing with. But he couldn't wait any longer. He wanted to at least hear her voice. While he drove into town from Bridgeton Pass to get a deli sandwich for his lunch one afternoon, he called Sara.

"Hello."

"Hi, Sara. It's Cole. How are things going?"

"Oh, Cole." Her tone was neutral.

He winced. "Sara? Is it a problem that I called you?"

"No, of course not. I guess I'm embarrassed that I haven't contacted you sooner. I never thanked you for all you did to help me after my mom's accident."

"How is she doing?"

"She's getting better slowly. Thanks for asking." Then she added, "Cole, have I ruined any chance of seeing you again?"

He let out a little laugh. "No, Sara, not at all. I do want to see you again but take the time you need. I'll be here, waiting. Call me when it's good for you."

"Thank you, Cole. For everything."

He disconnected and tossed his phone onto the

45

passenger seat in frustration. He wished they could have had just a bit more time together before her mother's accident happened. That would have eased his soul before letting out the tether as she needed him to do now. At least he still had some hold on ties to her at this point. Their time together that night, before Sara got the call about her mother's fall, was intense, erotic. But their time together was halted abruptly, before either of them was ready for the night to end. He felt as though he had suddenly fallen off a cliff two weeks prior and was still waiting to be rescued.

June 2010

He felt that he had been thrown a life-line when he saw Sara's name come up on his phone a week later.

"Would you consider having dinner with me soon?" she asked.

"Absolutely. Are you in Greenville?"

"I will be."

"I'll be there for business overnight Wednesday to Thursday. Can you wait two days?"

"Sure, the bistro at seven o'clock?"

"See you then."

Cole went to the pharmacy in town that evening. He dropped the box of condoms on the counter next to the register and reached for his wallet.

"Hmmm. Planning an evening of fun, are you?" a voice full of sarcasm asked from behind him.

Cole was used to the occasional harassment over buying condoms. It came with the territory when living in a small town. He had even harassed some of his own friends in the past. But it was 'special' harassment that evening.

"Hello, Laurie."

"That's a big box of condoms, Cole. Yee-haw, you go, cowboy!"

"Okay, then," he muttered. He didn't say anything when he saw her holding her intended purchase, a pregnancy test kit. He tried to cover a grin while he looked directly at her.

The color drained from her face, and she looked slightly panicked. "It's not for me."

"Oh," he said as if he believed her. He took his change and bag with the condoms from the cashier and left Laurie to contemplate Cole having sex with a new girlfriend and probably wishing she had gotten the opportunity to explain her purchase.

The Wednesday that Cole was to meet Sara at the bistro had been full with meetings and by the evening Cole was tired but looking forward to seeing Sara at dinner and even more of her after dinner. He got there first and waited for her at a table.

He watched her as she walked into the bistro wearing a simple light yellow sheath dress and tall pumps. He admired her curves and the sway of her hips. Cole stood as she approached their table and pulled her chair out for her. He fitted his body to hers for a brief hug and brushed her ear with his lips when he whispered hello. She placed her clutch bag on the table and allowed him to help push her chair in.

He sat across from her. She looked nervous and gave him a plastic smile. Cole felt the tension and his jaw tightened.

"What is it, Sara?"

Her eyes skittered over the table before she tilted her head at him with a questioning look.

"Tell me." His voice was demanding. The waiter then appeared to take their drink order. He steeled his eyes on her while the waiter took their order.

"It's fine, Cole. I'm just a bit tired," she offered.

It's fine, not I'm fine? He tried to calm himself. His phone rang, and he silenced it.

"How was work today?" she asked blandly.

"It was fine. I'm also fine."

She bit her bottom lip. The waiter delivered their drinks, then Cole dismissed him as they were not ready to place their food orders just yet. Sara looked at him over the edge of her glass as she took a large sip of her wine. He figured she needed fortification for whatever it was she was about say. When she didn't say anything, he asked, "How's your mother?"

"Actually, she's not doing as well as we hoped at home." Sara explained that her mother would require help from then on to manage. She had been having in-home nursing care and physical therapy but those were going to be stopping soon and her mother would still need to have help. "My boss recommended me for a position at a company in Columbia. I'm pretty sure I will get the job. I'm sorry, Cole, but I have to move back home and live with my mother. She won't accept living anywhere else but in her own home. She only has me and my sister. Our father passed away several years ago. My sister has a two-year-old daughter to care for and is pregnant again. Her husband is managing the farm. I'm the only one left to care for her."

Cole's heart sank. The hurt and worry in her eyes tore at him. Cole knew what it was like to care for elderly family members having helped his father care for Cole's grandparents until they passed. It would be difficult for her, and she would be doing it essentially alone. She'd be taking care of her mother and the house while working full-time. And then there was their new relationship. Apparently, she knew it was going to be difficult. She was breaking up with him. He could understand that, but he'd just found Sara, and he wasn't going to let her go.

"Sara, I still want to see you. I don't care about the distance."

"It's not just the distance, Cole."

"I know. This is going to be a lot for you. It will be hard to do. But I can help…"

"No. No. You're a wonderful guy, Cole, but this is my burden."

"And I want to help you with it."

"Please, Cole. Don't make this harder than it is. It's better to break this off now while it's still all so new."

"I don't know what it is, Sara, but I can't let you go. I won't."

"Don't…" Tears started to flow, and Sara grabbed her clutch and ran from the restaurant.

Cole was numb. He sat staring at the seat where she had just been sitting. The life-line dangled above his head just out of reach, taunting him.

Running in impossibly high heels was not working, especially when crying at the same time. Sara stopped outside the front door of the bistro to collect herself. She hoped Cole wasn't chasing after her. She rummaged in her clutch for tissues she had wisely stuffed into the bag before she left work, figuring she would need them for this meeting with Cole. Sara wiped the tears from her eyes and face, then stuffed the used tissue back into her bag.

The backseat of her car held bags of her clothes, enough to get her through several weeks at home with her mother. If this was what putting your big girl panties on was like, she wasn't a fan of it. Sara loved her mother. Of course, no one wants to see their parent sick and needing assistance. She would help her mother, no one else could right now and it was her mother who needed help. Just why did she have to meet Cole now? Couldn't she have met him at a better time? Sara thought about the potential happiness she could have if she could put all her attention on getting to know Cole. He was such a nice guy. He was caring, gentle, thoughtful, and so incredibly handsome. His thick brown hair felt so nice when she'd run her fingers through it. She had fallen mesmerized into his gaze many times, admiring the gold flecks in the deep chocolate brown of his eyes. She wanted to explore his body. His tight T-shirts and jeans hinted of a gorgeous body beneath, but she wanted to feel it, explore it, and know every inch of it. Breaking it off before she grew too attached to him was the best thing, the only thing, she could have done. It would be better this way. But Sara had been ready to meet someone to have a long-term relationship with, and Cole seemed to have been a good candidate. Would she ever meet someone else that she would want to be in a long-term relationship with? She had to think that she would, but there was always the possibility that she may not.

Cole threw himself into his work the next day in attempt to stop thinking about Sara. The sight of the empty bed when he went into his hotel room last evening had reignited his anger and his frustration had yet to dissipate. He was glad when Jeff was able to meet him for golf later that afternoon.

"So, what's going on?" Jeff asked as they approached their third hole.

"Life."

"Ah. A woman's behind this, am I right?"

"You sure are." Cole let out a big sigh.

"What'd you do?"

"Fuck you, Jeff. It's like I said, life's gotten in our way."

"Meaning…"

"Her mom's sick, she's the only one who can rearrange her life to take care of her, so she's moving back to their farm outside of Columbia."

Jeff whistled. "Wow. That sucks. Columbia's two hours away from where you live and now she's a woman with baggage. Do I know her?"

"Sara Thompkins, the woman I dumped beer over on St. Patty's Day."

"Ouch. She's a babe. I hope you got a piece of ass at least."

"Nice, Jeff."

"Sorry, but that's one—"

"Shut the fuck up!"

"You've really got feelings for her, don't you?"

"You think?"

"Well, don't give up then if you think she's worth it."

"She broke up with me. She's got too much on her plate to deal with me too. She'll have to come find me if her situation changes and she thinks I'm worth it."

"Yeah, that's a good plan." Jeff rolled his eyes.

July 2010

Luckily, Cole tried to convince himself, there was a prospective foal for purchase which would give him work to help keep his mind off of Sara that summer. Deep down he knew no amount of work would help him accomplish that. It was all he had to focus on at the moment.

"She's special," Cole said. "She has that 'something' about her."

"She's very beautiful," James added.

J.P. passed the portrait to William. "She has very expressive eyes. I like that."

William took the portrait from J.P. "So, we agree. Cole, draw up the contract. Bridgeton Pass will purchase the foal, Celestra." Everyone nodded in agreement.

51

Manuel, J.P. and the farm's veterinarian had recommended Bridgeton Pass acquire Celestra a few months prior. William had been considering the foal and now they would make an offer to purchase her.

Cole caught up to J.P. in the hallway outside the conference room in Bridgeton Pass's administration building. "So, looks like you're gonna have a good horse to work with soon."

"I'm looking forward to it. It's very exciting." J.P. rubbed his hands together in anticipation. Cole appreciated that their apprentice trainer had such enthusiasm for his work. Their farm was family owned and the family worked hard. It was good to know J.P. was working for the same goals as the family. Cole knew that his father had his concerns about J.P. in terms of any intentions the trainer may have for Audra, Cole's sister, but Cole didn't see J.P. as any real threat. Like any good businessman, however, he had to keep his mind open to the possibility that J.P. could be a very real threat to the family farm.

Passing James' office as he walked down the hall, he asked if James would be going to the main house to get lunch today.

"Yes, but not just yet. I'll meet you over there," James said from where he sat behind his desk.

Cole entered the kitchen in the main house to find Audra on her hands and knees picking up grapes off the kitchen floor. She looked up to her brother. "I dropped the grapes," she said simply. The bowl that the grapes had obviously been in was on the floor beside her. He helped pick up the last of the grapes, then went to the pantry to get the items he wanted to make a sandwich. Just as he stepped out of the pantry he witnessed Audra attempting to place the full bowl of grapes on the kitchen table only to misjudge and drop the bowl again. She growled in frustration and stamped her foot, smashing one of the rogue grapes into the kitchen floor. As Cole helped her gather the grapes back into the bowl one more time, James entered the kitchen.

"Oh, snot, what are you doing?" James exclaimed, using his nickname for his little sister.

Cole shot a glare at James, warning him to lay off of Audra. "What are you so nervous about, sweetie?" Cole asked.

Audra explained that she had accepted a date to go to the County Fair from a guy in her class. She obviously wasn't excited about going, and Cole knew she struggled with going on a date with someone other than J.P. Cole tried his best to support his sister by pointing out her options. Unfortunately, James jumped in trying to help as well, mentioning that J.P. would be too busy for her to bother anyway, just as their father walked into the kitchen.

"Go on the date, Audra," William ordered.

Cole dropped his head in defeat. He would have essentially told her the same thing but had been trying to do so with care. Audra ignored the bowl full of grapes on the floor and left the kitchen. He didn't blame her for giving up.

Going to the County Fair was a big deal throughout high school, Cole reminisced later that evening. His first kiss had been at a County Fair. He kissed Ellen Landon behind the giant pretzel truck when he was fifteen. He had to admit, for a first kiss, it had been a good one. The memory only made him think of how much he missed Sara. It had been only ten days since she left him in the bistro in Greenville. He hadn't stopped thinking of her since. He doubted that she'd done anything other than tend to her mother and work at her new job. She was undoubtedly working toward being burnt out real soon.

He had to call her. He was becoming more moody and difficult to be around. Much of the time, he didn't even like being around himself. He couldn't imagine trying to forget her and find someone else. He'd never had trouble sending a woman off on her own way after a few dates. This didn't make sense. His thoughts kept coming back to this woman. Whatever it was about her, he didn't want to try to analyze any further, especially if she wasn't going to talk to him. So he decided to call and see what happened.

"Hello," came her stern greeting through the phone.

"Hi, Sara. It's Cole." He paused but heard nothing. "I know you want me to forget about you, but I can't." Still he heard nothing. "Sara?"

It was a long moment before Sara spoke. "Cole..." She had pleaded. She couldn't forget about him either but needed to.

"No, Sara. I don't mean to add to all the stress you're dealing with. I just wanted to call and hear your voice, ask how you're doing. Can you give me just these few moments?"

"Why? You need to find someone else, someone more accessible. I can't be that for you right now. And I don't want to be reminded of what I chose to give up."

"It doesn't have to be all or nothing. You could call when you need someone to listen. And if I call and it's not a good time for you, I won't mind that you tell me so. Can we at least give it a try, Sara? You have to know that I care about you. I don't make just any girl come in a booth at the diner." He heard Sara laugh and wished he could watch her blush as he knew she was.

"Okay, Cole. I'll give this a try. I just can't promise anything."

"I don't want you to make me any promises."

"Thank you."

"So, how are you, Sara?" he asked again.

"I don't even know how I feel. I suppose as I develop a routine with my mom it will get easier. I have to do or at least help her with everything plus cooking, shopping, cleaning and then starting a new job."

"Does Beth help any?"

"When she can, but she's got her hands full and is tired a lot because of the pregnancy. She's dropped off a casserole that she made and came by to pick up the house a little on Saturday."

"Good."

"I'm sorry, Cole, but I've got to hang up and get back to my mom. Though I'd much rather talk to you."

"There's no need to be sorry. Do what you need to. I'll talk to you again soon."

"Thanks. Bye, Cole."

"Good night, Sara Thompkins," he said just as he had said the night he met her.

The week had been a long, stressful one at work for Cole. He wanted nothing more to stop for a bit and call Sara, to hear her voice, let it wrap around him and soothe him. When Cole finally got to stop and call Sara that evening he fell onto his bed with a sigh. Lying on the comforter, he propped a pillow behind his head and dialed her number.

"Hey, Cole," she answered.

"Hey. Is this a good time to call?" He wanted to be sure Sara wasn't in the middle of something important and that his call didn't make her feel overwhelmed.

"At the moment it is." He heard her sigh and she sounded tired.

"Yeah, what were you doing?"

"Putting a load of laundry in the washing machine. Exciting, huh?"

"Are you kidding? All that lacy underwear and lingerie."

Sara laughed. "More like cotton briefs you could easily fly on a flag pole they're so large."

"Thanks for that visual about your mother's underwear."

"I'm talking about mine!"

"Oh, honey, I've seen your underwear. They were all lace and strings that graciously adorned your sensuous curves."

"Right. You did see that set." Her heart sank at the memory of all that they had anticipated the evening her mother went to the hospital.

"Hey, don't sound sad. Just think, you'll show me them again next time we're together. Seeing you in them once could never be enough."

"I would like to do more than strip them off for you, though. I'm going to Greenville on Wednesday, for work, but it will be for just a few hours and during the day.

"Yeah, so, I'll meet you at the hotel downtown before you drive back."

"Hmmm, that's the best offer I've received...ever."

Cole could hear Sara's mom in the background. "Coming, Mom! I gotta go, Cole."

"So, I'll see you Wednesday."

"Yes. As much of me as you want." Her voice breathy, she hung up.

On Wednesday, Cole sat at the desk in the hotel suite with his laptop, doing work. Closing the things he had been working on, he logged off his computer. He was expecting Sara any moment. Briefly, he thought maybe she wouldn't show. But he doubted that, she had sounded like she needed him as much as he needed her. He knew for Sara this was going to be sex for stress relief. He was okay with it, no strings and all that. Besides, he was willing to help her out. It wasn't like some mid-afternoon sex wasn't going to helpful to his state of well-being as well.

He could see when he opened the door at her soft

knock that she had lost some weight. She stepped into the suite and dropped her purse on an upholstered chair. Cole closed the door and pulled her to him, then just held her for a long moment, until he felt her relax in his arms. "That's it, baby. Just relax. I'll take good care of you." He kissed her tenderly on her temple, then stepped back to look at her. "Can I get you anything?"

"Just you." She closed her eyes and took a big, cleansing breath.

He took her hand, and they walked to the bedroom.

"Cole, I hope you understand that I can't promise you anything. Today is—"

"Shhh. We already talked about this. I don't want any promises from you." He pulled her blouse from the waistband of her skirt. "I'll take care of you. All you need to do is let yourself feel." He made a trail of soft kisses from behind her ear and down neck.

"I can do that."

Cole had been waiting for this moment with Sara since St. Patty's Day, since he first laid eyes on her. It took everything he had to force himself to be tender and slow with her, knowing that was what she really needed right now, when all he really wanted was to be inside her and soon. He unbuttoned her blouse, the bottom edges of which he had freed from her skirt already, and let it fall off her shoulders.

"Are you on the pill, Sara?" He traced a finger down her arm.

"Yes. Are you clean?"

"Yes. Are you?"

"Yes. Can I trust you?"

He looked into her eyes, hoping she'd trust him. "I'm clean, Sara, but I do have condoms with me and will use one if you want me to."

"No. I want to feel you." That was all Sara wanted

right now, to just feel. To feel with such intensity that let her forget everything else, if even just for a little while.

They were putting a lot of trust in each other but with her last request she would get no argument from him. He noticed that she was wearing the same lacy underwear that she had been wearing the night they shared dinner at her apartment, the night their erotic evening was abruptly halted. A smile crossed his lips as he dragged a finger across the sheer lace of the bra over her nipple. His finger stopped there to circle the rosy tip. Moaning softly, she arched her back, thrusting her breast firmly into his hand. With his free hand he unclasped her bra and drew it away from her body before dropping it on the floor. His eyes took her in, admiring how beautiful she was. He cupped her breasts with both hands and massaged them gently. Cole loved breasts, and he truly admired Sara's breasts. They were generous and perfect. He put his lips on one nipple, pulled it into his mouth and suckled using long slow draws. She let her head fall back and, as he had told her to do, she let herself just feel. He could sense the tension easing from her body. Cole slid his hands over her ribs, and down her sides to grasp and softly squeeze her buttocks. From there his hands slid to the zipper of her skirt, and he pulled it down.

Wanting to feel her skin on his, she began unbuttoning his shirt as he pushed her skirt down over her hips. She pushed the sides of his shirt open. Sara took time to admire his sculpted chest and was eager to feel her bare chest against the wiry brown curls covering his. She closed her eyes and let him pull her to him, putting her arms around his neck. He pressed her breasts snug against his body with his large palm against her back, slid his other arm around her low back, and buried his face in her hair. For a moment they just held each other close. Cole felt a slight shudder run through Sara's body. "You're okay, Sara," he assured her. Kissing her earlobe, he took in her scent, a mixture of warm amber and a smell all her own.

Cole released his embrace to slide her panties down, let her step out of them, then scooped her into his arms to lay her across the bed. While kicking off his boots and socks, he unbuttoned his jeans. "Let me." Sara's voice was small and sweet for the task she requested. He smiled at her and let his hands drop to his sides. Sara rolled onto her side and sat up to grab his jeans at the outsides of his knees and pull them down. She was eye level with the bulge in his boxers and could feel the heat emanating from his body. Sara looked up at him as she pulled the material of his boxers out and over him to slide them down his legs. Having stripped him of his clothes, she looked at him as he stood before her, stiff and erect. He was gorgeous.

"That's all I can handle right now, Sara. You touch me again and I'm not going to be able to help but come all over you." He nearly did when she looked up at him just then. She leaned back to lie on the bed and Cole joined her at her side. "You're so gorgeous, Sara," he whispered as he pushed a length of her hair away from her face. Her face softened into an appreciative smile.

"Kiss me," she said, and so he did. They shared a deep, sensuous kiss while her hands explored the muscular terrain of his back and his tight ass. He nudged her legs apart and slid a finger along her folds. As soon as he felt the slickness that was there, he grabbed her wrists and pulled her arms to hold them in his one hand over her head.

"I can't wait, Sara," he growled.

"Please," she begged, and then he heard her gasp as he slid into her.

"Oh my God. You feel so good." His words escaped between heavy breaths. He was in, his full length. He slid back in her warm chamber, then thrust again. He felt her breathing become heavier, and slid fully into her once more. A strangled voice called out his name. She turned her head from one side to the other against the pillow. "Please," she begged. He pulled out and found her clit with his finger before he slammed back into her. She wrapped her legs around him and rocked her hips in rhythm with him. His finger played over her clit, and he felt her tightening around him. She grabbed the sheets, gripping them into her fists and with sweet release he felt her go over the edge. The feel of her spasming around him and the beautiful vision of her coming beneath him triggered his own orgasm. He collapsed over her, kissed her cheek and rolled his weight off of her. "Are you okay?" he asked.

"Absolutely." She had been staring at the ceiling, letting her heart rate return to normal. She felt a mixture of pure bliss as she floated back to Earth, yet knew she was now ruined as far as sex with anyone else. No one else could compare to that. She wasn't sure, at first, if the words came from her. "Cole, that was the most amazing sex I've ever had."

He smiled at her. "Stay with me here a little longer then. We'll do it again."

He could see goose bumps forming on her arms. He pulled the sheet over to cover them. She didn't tell him that the goose bumps were not because she was cold, and the thought of that scared her. This couldn't go anywhere. She didn't have time in her life right now to get comfortable in a relationship. She shot up into sitting on the bed, then stood and began to gather her clothes. Cole watched her moving frantically, picking up and sorting through her clothes among his on the floor. He slid to the edge of the bed and stood beside her, then folded his body around hers. "Sara? Hey, no promises, remember?"

"I know, Cole. This just scared the shit out of me all

of a sudden. I've got to go."

He tightened his embrace on her. "No, not until you calm down." He rested his chin on the top of her head. But Sara squirmed to be let go of. Her heart rate and breathing didn't slow. He let her pull away from him but did not let go. "Hey, look at me," he spoke tenderly.

Her blue eyes turned to look at him. "Will you text me when you get home so that I know you made it safe?"

"Sure," she said, though her smile was tentative.

A few hours later, Cole received a text from Sara.

Sara: *Home safe. TY for taking care of me 2day. Not many guys R so nice.*

Cole: *TY for letting me know U R safe. I only treated U as U deserved. G'nite ST.*

Cole understood Sara's need for a no strings attached attitude with all she had going on in her life. Heck, he wanted to get to know her but wasn't ready to commit to anyone at that point in his life either. He just wished she had less stressors so that their being together wasn't one of them. Though he had known that their being together was the easiest of her stressors to take off her plate, he hadn't been able to leave her. Cole had waited a few days before calling her again, but she hadn't answered her phone that evening or the other two evenings he had tried calling her thereafter. She had been shutting him out. He had left messages asking her to call when she was able, but he hadn't thought she would be calling him back. He had really come to dislike this mother of Sara's that he had never met.

Sara enjoyed being with Cole. She thought she enjoyed it too much. She knew he understood she couldn't promise him anything more than something superficial but what they had didn't feel all that superficial to her. It was more than just sex. He took the time to understand her needs, then had been kind enough to give her what she needed. And so she couldn't take his calls or call him back. It was ridiculous, when she thought about it, that her life had become such that she couldn't deal with a guy who treated her well and won't deal with someone who would treat her poorly. So basically, that told her that she shouldn't be with anyone. Then why was it so difficult to let him go? She had so much to do, she had told herself, that she wouldn't have time to think about him. Nonetheless, she thought about him all the time. Sara decided the next time Cole called, if he did, she would tell him she couldn't see him anymore, again. But she would tell him more firmly this time, because she meant it.

Two weeks after their afternoon of incredible sex and five days after he had left his last phone message, Sara got a text.

Cole: *Hey ST. Plz don't shut me out.*

Sara: *I have to. So plz stop seeking me out.*

Cole: *No. I can't.*

Sara: *I M not asking.*

Cole: *I M not listening.*

Sara: *I know & U R driving me crazy.*

Cole: *So, I'll call U soon.*

Sara: *&$%#@*

Cole: *LOL. XOXO*

Okay, so I have no willpower, Sara thought, *not when it comes to Cole Becker.*

James' car was in the shop for maintenance work. So, when he asked Cole for a ride to the public recreation fields in town to attend a polo club meeting, Cole said yes.

"I can catch a ride home from one of the guys so you'll just have to drop me off."

"All right. I've got nothing else to do."

James thanked his brother for the ride once they had reached the fields and closed the door to Cole's car. Cole remained sitting in his car with it in park. He wasn't ready to go home for the evening but wasn't sure what he wanted to do. After a few minutes he put his car into drive, left the public fields' parking lot and drove to the coffee shop in downtown.

There were only two other people in the coffee shop. A woman sat on one of the couches by the front window, drinking tea and reading a book. By the far wall a teenage boy wearing ear buds sat at a table and studied from a history text book. Cole ordered a strong brewed coffee, black, at the counter. He handed the barista a ten dollar bill.

"Cole? Cole Becker?"

Cole turned toward the voice coming from the direction of the shop's entrance. He hadn't heard the door open.

"Ellen?"

"Yes. Wow, I haven't seen you in forever, Cole!" She stepped toward him, holding his gaze.

At fifteen, Ellen Landon had been the first girl Cole had kissed. Other than uncomfortable chance meetings in the high school hallways during the remainder of their freshman year together in high school they hadn't seen each other. Ellen had dated one of Cole's friends, Pete, during their junior and senior years. She was a leggy brunette with a friendly smile and bright blue eyes. He remembered that she had come to some parties with Pete and that Pete had taken her to the prom. Cole wasn't sure what had happened to Ellen after high school graduation. He hadn't seen her until now.

"Not since graduation. How have you been?"

"Good. Pete and I went to Duke, but he transferred to Ohio State after our first year. I haven't heard much from him since. What about you?"

"I went to Furman in Greenville and have been working for my dad. Want to join me at a table?"

"Sure. I've got a little time. I'm on my way to pick up my mom. She's at the salon getting her hair done. Let me order my coffee, and I'll meet you at a table."

Cole chose a small café table not far from the shop's entrance where Ellen joined him.

"What brings you into town?"

"My mom's sixtieth birthday is this weekend. My sister still lives in Carnegie but my brother will be coming back to town for the weekend. He's been living in Colorado."

"Yeah, I see Lindsey now and again around town. She said that you're living in Pennsylvania."

"I am. I have a great job and it's okay living there."

"You don't sound too excited about it." He watched the creases form at the corners of her eyes when she smiled. Ellen had a great smile.

"Well, it's somewhat boring where I live. I plan to stay another year, then start looking to move on." She pushed a lock of her long hair behind her ear.

"I see." Cole couldn't help but be mesmerized by Ellen's smile. Maybe that's why he had wanted to kiss her so badly at fifteen. She had great lips. As if on cue, she licked her bottom lip.

"So, you think you'll stay in Carnegie?"

"Yeah, it's home, and I enjoy the work at the farm."

Ellen looked at her watch. "Oh my, sorry, Cole, I've got to run. I've got to pick up my mom, you know?"

"Sure. It was great to see you, Ellen."

"It was great to see you too. Take care." She gave a little wave as she walked out of the shop.

Cole sighed and took a last sip from his coffee cup. It was good to see Ellen, he thought. She had matured and was pretty. He couldn't help but notice the carefree attitude she seemed to have. Cole began to think that maybe a relationship with Sara wasn't worth it. He hadn't really wanted a woman who had baggage. Sara's had been in the form of a sick elderly mother. Cole had lived that nightmare of being a caregiver. He didn't want to live that way again through his girlfriend. It was something he'd have to think about.

* * *

The phone in Cole's office rang. He looked at the caller ID to see that it was Melissa, Bridgeton Pass's office assistant, calling.

"Yes, Melissa?"

"You have a visitor."

"I'll be right there." Melissa usually turned away a sales person who came around without an appointment. Cole wasn't sure who could be in the lobby waiting. He was more than pleased when he saw that it was Sara. "Hey there!" he said.

Her smile was bright and genuine. "Hi, Cole." She grabbed his hand and squeezed it in an effort to touch him in some way, any way. "I was out this way for work. I hope you don't mind that I stopped in unannounced."

"Not at all. Have you had lunch?" he asked, though it was already two o'clock.

"Yes. And I don't have all that much time…"

"Come on. We'll sit outside." Cole guided Sara toward the door with his hand at her lower back, gave a nod to assure Melissa had heard where he would be, then held the door open. Outside the administration building was a wooden bench. Cole ran the back of his hand lightly over Sara's cheek after they had sat down. "How are you?"

"Okay." She shrugged.

"Why didn't let me know you'd be out this way? I could have met you in Greenville."

"I wasn't sure how much time I was going to have after I completed the work I went there for. So, I figured if I had any extra time I would come out here and surprise you." Actually, Sara didn't say it, but she was afraid of how her heart would feel when it came time to leave Cole had they met at the hotel again.

"Oh." It made no sense, but he didn't know what else to say. Her coming out to the farm from Greenville added an extra hour to her commute back to Columbia and there was always the chance that he may not have been in the office.

"The farm is beautiful." She looked around at the large spread. There was no comparison with the small, shabby farm her family owned. Sara's father had died several years ago, and though Sara's brother-in-law tried to help maintain the farm, he was only able to do so marginally with both time and money being tight. She tried not to think about how it was falling down around them.

"May I offer you a quick tour?" Cole asked.

Sara accepted. Cole held her hand as he brought her around to the various barns and pastures. He introduced her to any hands they encountered as his girlfriend. Both

James and Audra were at school, so he couldn't introduce her to them, and he decided not to make Sara endure meeting his father. His and Sara's relationship was not at a point where he felt he needed to introduce her to his father just yet. He led Sara back to her car after the tour, assuming that she would need to leave. He opened her door for her.

"Sara, thanks so much for making the effort to come out and visit. I can't tell how wonderful it was to see you this afternoon." He didn't want to make her feel guilty mentioning that he would have preferred to have met her at the hotel again in Greenville. But hell, he was going to get at least a kiss before she left. Cole grabbed her waist when she stepped toward her car door that he stood next to holding it open. He landed his mouth on hers and felt no resistance. No, he felt her run her tongue along his bottom lip and heard a soft moan. He felt her open hands on his chest begin to knead his skin. Why had she denied herself all that he could have given her if she had arranged to meet with him today? She had kept as much distance as she could, wanting to see him in public at his office and not wanting to put herself in a private place with him where neither could resist the other. He stopped their heated kiss and dotted her face with soft caresses from his lips instead. "Sara, you need me as much as I need you. Not today. You have to get going. But soon, okay?" he spoke softly and cupped her cheek with his hand.

She let out a big sigh. "I don't know. I don't see me having any free time soon…"

"Shhh. Don't worry, we'll work it out."

She wanted to believe him, she just didn't see it happening. Cole nudged her to get into her car, then closed the door when she did. Through her open car window he told Sara they would keep in touch and wished her a safe ride home. Luckily, today it would still be light by the time she got home, so he didn't need to worry so much about her as when she drove the long distance in the dark. Cole stood in the driveway watching her car drive away until he could see it no more.

He returned to his office and a moment later James was at his door. He hadn't noticed that James was home from school and had come into the office. His brother leaned against the door frame with his arms folded over his chest. "Who was that masterpiece of womanly beauty?" James asked.

"Ah," Cole replied. "Sara Thompkins, I spilled beer over her." When he looked up from his desk at the confused expression on James' face, he clarified, "St. Patty's Day."

Their relationship was turning out to be quite a bit like a roller coaster ride. Cole hated roller coasters. Nonetheless, he decided he would just go along for the ride. Secretly, he hoped her mother would be flung out of the coaster's seat just as it crested a steep rise. He worried that, more likely, he would eventually just become bored with his relationship with Sara, like he had with Laurie. But he knew he couldn't do as he had done with his relationship with Laurie, just end the ride because he thought he'd become too bored.

August-September 2010

Cole had felt like a kid at Christmas when Sara told him that her sister agreed to stay with their mom for a weekend so Sara could enjoy a weekend free of familial responsibilities. He invited Sara to stay at the farm, and they decided on a weekend. On the Saturday morning of the weekend that they had agreed upon Sara arrived around ten o'clock and parked in the circle drive. She met

Cole in the barn as he instructed her to do. Also, as he instructed, she wore jeans and boots.

"Hey, sugar." He gave her a firm embrace and a hungry kiss when she entered the barn.

"Ah, I thought we might be going riding," she said. Two horses were tacked and ready for a trail ride.

"Sure are. Did you bring a hat?"

By the reaction on Sara's face, he gathered she hadn't, so Cole grabbed a hat hanging along a wall in the barn and placed it roughly on her head.

"Yuck!" Sara immediately took the hat off and held it away from her. "Whose hat is this?"

"Doesn't matter, just put it on."

Sara returned the hat to where Cole had taken it off the wall. She didn't hide her disgust and even irritation on her face. She returned to where the horses were waiting to find him already mounted.

Cole led them on a trail ride on the Bridgeton Pass property. The trails cut through land thick with tall trees. Shards of sunlight pierced the trees canopy in places, creating an ethereal feel. The light drenched the banks of the stream, however. Along the portion of the stream that they had come to, large boulders provided spots where Sara and Cole sat for some time. Their horses drank from the stream and grazed while they listened to the water as it cascaded over fallen tree limbs and other rocks.

"It's very peaceful here."

"Mmm."

"Do you ride out here often?"

"Yes. My sister, Audra, and I ride almost daily. This is one trail that we take quite often."

"How old is your sister?"

"Seventeen."

"You're close. That's nice. I wish I had an older brother but only if he had been nice."

Cole laughed. "She's a great person. We're close. More so than most siblings, I'm sure. I helped my dad with a lot after my mom died. Audra was only five at the time, so I've always looked out for her."

"Family's important."

Cole was glad to know Sara felt the same way. He filed that information away.

From there, they followed the trail out of the woods to where the view was of the mountains not far in the distance. These were views that Sara missed because her family lived on the flat land to the south of Columbia.

Two of the farm hands took over the horses when she and Cole returned from their ride. Cole explained that there was a smaller house, called the small house, on the property which had been where his grandparents had lived when they were alive.

"Let's grab your bag from your car. I'll take you to the house. You can shower there."

The idea of a shower appealed to Sara after being in the hot sun all morning. She decided not to mention this to Cole, given she had not brought her hat or worn the one he told her to wear. He led her on a short walk to the quaint house and let her in.

"We'll sleep in the master bedroom. It's on the right at the top of the stairs. Shower in the bathroom in that room. Be ready in twenty minutes."

"Yes, sir," Sara muttered and threw her bag over her shoulder in disbelief.

"Is there a problem?" Cole asked.

"No," she said tentatively and then asked him, "Do you have a problem?"

"Only if you're not ready in twenty minutes. We're going to get some lunch, and I'm starving," he said blandly, then added. "I'm going to use the bathroom in my room in the main house. I'll meet you at my car in the driveway."

"Sounds like a reasonable plan." She tried to keep the sarcasm from her voice.

In the shower Sara tried to reason whether it was just her or did Cole seem to not be his usual easygoing self. It could just be that he was hungry, but she doubted it.

At the diner in town Sara was happy to see that no one was sitting in "their booth" and began to walk toward it. Cole grabbed her hand, led her to another table and sat down.

"Don't you want to sit in 'our booth'?" Sara asked.

Cole's expression was cold. "This is fine here."

"I know, I just thought—"

"We're fine here, Sara," he commanded.

Sara backed off but couldn't help feeling irritated with Cole's mood. After all, this was her one weekend away from all her responsibilities so that she could relax and have fun. And furthermore, he had been the one to invite her to come out here to his place.

"Cole, will you be in this sour mood all weekend because I'd rather not stay if that's the case?"

He furrowed his brow and returned to looking over the menu. The man had only lived here his whole life, she couldn't imagine that he didn't know the menu by heart.

Cole didn't know what had come over him. He should be happy that Sara was visiting for the weekend. It's not that he wasn't happy that she was here…what was it? He liked taking her to dinner at a restaurant. He liked talking to her on the phone, emailing, texting and even sexting with her. And there certainly was no problem with their compatibility in bed.

"Cole?" Sara was waving her hand in front of his face.

"What? I'm sorry."

"I just wanted to know if you wanted to share some fries with me."

"Yeah, sure."

Once their orders were taken, Sara sat forward in her seat in the booth and folded her hands on the table. "Talk to me. What's going on? You were certainly in deep thought and never answered me."

"I don't know, Sara. Can we just forget about it?" Cole didn't want to dwell on his mood.

"Not if this is how your mood is going to be all weekend. I don't need this."

What she said hit him. *No, Sara doesn't need this.* Whatever was causing his bad mood, she didn't need to take the brunt of it. She had enough going on and didn't need to deal with his brooding. *That's why she's here.*

Oh shit, he thought, *she is here, isn't she? At my place...all weekend...that's what's bothering me, isn't it? Oh great. No strings attached, remember?* He didn't want to accept that it was his own damn heart that he needed to worry about.

Sara stood as if to leave. Not that she had a car to leave with since Cole drove them into town.

"Sit down, Sara." He hadn't meant the annoyance he heard in his tone, so he gently grasped both her hands. "Sara, please, sit with me."

She lowered herself slowly back to sitting. The sadness on her face tore at his heart. She looked at him expectantly.

"Sara, I ..."

Suellen placed their plates on the table. "Here you go," she said and reached into her apron pocket to produce a bottle of ketchup and two straws before leaving.

"Listen Cole, if this is not working I can just get my things from the guest house—"

"No Sara, I want you to stay. I want to be with you this weekend."

"You have a funny way of showing it."

Her words hit him because he knew she was right. "I'm sorry. I've been an ass ever since you drove in this morning." He brought his head up to look at her.

"I'm listening."

Cole liked her I-don't-take-no-shit attitude. The corners of his mouth flinched.

"It's just that I suddenly felt...I don't know...sort of overwhelmed, maybe. We've never spent more than a few hours together, and now not only are spending the whole weekend together and we're doing it on my turf. I know, I invited you here. I didn't know I was going to feel this way, but I'm getting over the initial shock."

Sara pushed her food around on the plate. She wasn't hungry any longer.

"Please, give me a chance. I really do want you here this weekend. Please, stay."

Remembering the moment of panic that she had after their afternoon tryst in a hotel suite in Greenville, Sara couldn't help but feel that she should give him a second chance. "I'll stay."

A big smile came over Cole's face. "Thanks, Sara." He let out the breath he hadn't realized that he had been holding.

The panic that Cole initially experienced during Sara's visit that weekend subsided after their talk at the diner. They enjoyed their time together thereafter. Cole grilled steaks and vegetables for dinner. They ate outside on the patio at the small house and then relaxed there after they had finished eating. Cole pointed out the constellations of stars that he was familiar with in the night sky. Together they enjoyed wine until the bottle was empty. Then Cole ran a bath for Sara in the deep claw foot tub in the master bath.

Sara laughed when she walked into the bathroom wearing only a robe that Cole had provided her with. She had never seen so many bubbles in a tub. Not certain that she would fit in the tub with the amount of bubbles that were in it, she stepped cautiously over the tub's high wall. Slowly, she sank through the layer of bubbles and sighed when she felt the warm water beneath envelope her. Sara lay still in the tub, rested her head on the edge and closed her eyes. Moments later, she heard Cole enter the bathroom.

"I'm never getting out of this tub."

"You'll wrinkle up something awful."

"I don't care." Sara laughed.

Cole kneeled beside the tub. He submerged a wash cloth into the warm water, squeezed some body wash onto it and guided Sara to lean forward. With long, gentle strokes, he ran the soapy wash cloth over the creamy, smooth skin of her back, then up over her shoulders. There he paused to drop the wash cloth into the water and knead her shoulders. Sara moaned as she felt the tension being massaged away. She held her eyes closed, breathed in the soft lavender scent of the body wash Cole used and let herself drift off into a relaxed state. Soft butterfly kissed landed along a trail from her shoulder to behind her ear, causing Sara to shiver despite the warm cocoon she sat in. She felt Cole's breath against her skin as he spoke.

"Thank you for staying and giving me another chance today."

Sara nodded.

"It came on all of a sudden."

"You were scared."

"Yes."

"Like what happened to me the afternoon we met at the hotel in Greenville. It came on all of a sudden and scared the shit out of me."

"I guess so. I think I started feeling an overwhelming sense of responsibility."

"For what?"

"I'm not sure. Your happiness, maybe. What if this weekend flopped and you left?"

"You were scared that I'll distance myself again."

"Yeah. We both want no strings attached but that doesn't mean I'm okay with losing contact with you. Keeping in touch lets me know you're still alive. It doesn't mean anything more than that."

"It means that you care."

"Yeah, I guess I do."

"And that scares me."

"My giving a shit about you scares you?"

"Yes."

"Well, it's a chance that I'm taking then 'cause I'm not going to stop caring about you."

"The water's starting to cool. I think I'll get out of the tub now."

Cole helped Sara step out of the tub safely. With a large, soft towel he gently dried her off, wrapped her in it and simply held her for a long while.

On Sunday evening Sara packed up her things to leave. The reality was she had to return to her childhood home and care for her sick, elderly mother. How long would this go on? *I'm twenty-three years old, for God's sake. I don't want to have to do this.* Sara knew she loved her mother, she just didn't like having to care for her to this extent. Despite her parents having been older than most, her mother had cared for her and her sister so well growing up. It was her turn to care for her mother, right?

"Ready, beautiful?" Cole took the bag from Sara's hand to carry it for her.

Sara couldn't believe the words that left her mouth. "I don't want to go."

Cole licked his lips, put the bag down, and pulled Sara into a hug. He kissed her gently on her lips, picked up her bag, and grabbed hold of her hand. "Come on," he said quietly. He led her to her car and helped her in. He deposited her bag in the backseat, then leaned his crossed forearms on the open driver's window. "You are the strongest woman I know. I wish this wasn't what you had to do right now with your life. I can't take it all away and make it better, though God knows I would if I could. I'll help in any way I can, though. Remember that, Sara."

Sara couldn't speak. Her eyes welled up, and she nodded. There were so many emotions that she was feeling, anger, frustration, fear, exhaustion and something like what she thought might be love. No, she was just tired and feeling sentimental. She didn't have time for love. Why did he have to care? She put her car in drive and drove away.

Sara had plenty of time to think during her two hour drive back to her family's farm. When she arrived home, she left her bag to unpack the next day, lay on her bed, and texted Cole.

Sara: I M home safe. I enjoyed the wkend. Wish we could spend every wkend 2gether.

Cole: I know U do, me 2. We'll get our someday, Sara.

Sara: Our someday...that sounds nice. Wish I could kiss U.

Cole: I want to kiss U 2 & more.

Sara: G'night Cole.

Cole: G'night ST.

October 2010

Cole and Sara continued to call, text or see each other as Sara's schedule allowed. Occasionally, Sara's mother went to bed early enough that Sara could work in a phone call to Cole before she could no longer stay awake and had to call it a night. It was during one of those calls that Sara made to Cole when she could tell that something wasn't right.

"What's bothering you, Cole?"

"Ah, I'm just feeling bad for my little sister, Audra. I've always been rather protective of her since our mom died. Anyway, she and our apprentice trainer, his name's J.P. Ryan, like each other, but my dad won't allow them to date."

"Why not?" Sara asked.

"Well, our trainer is pretty important to our success. J.P.'s apprenticing right now but actually his apprenticeship will be over after this coming Fall Race season. Then our long-time trainer, Manuel Rodriguez, will officially retire next summer. The farm will have put five years and a lot of money into training J.P. for the position, and he's really talented. So, the fear is if a relationship between them doesn't work out, we could lose J.P., all the time and money associated with training him, and we would have to start our search for a new trainer all over again. Then there's risk for any problems that may harm our reputation and so on."

"How old is this guy?"

"J.P.'s twenty-two."

"Wow, do you think this guy would really blow all the time he's put into training for what sounds like a prestigious position if he wasn't serious about your sister?"

"Well, Audra was telling me that she and J.P. haven't really had a whole lot of opportunity to spend time together as a couple. I mean, granted they've known each other since Audra was twelve, but because my father won't let them date and he has had J.P. traveling to a lot to races, they haven't got to get to know each on this other level. She just feels that she wants to have the opportunity to explore the possibility of a relationship between them."

"Hmm…both sides have pretty good points, huh?"

"Yeah, I won't take a side. It just kills me to see my sister so sad when she's usually so full of life. She's a really good person, Sara, and so sweet, but this has been really hard for her."

"You care a lot about her," Sara concluded.

"I wonder if I care too much. It's just so difficult to see her in pain. A while ago I watched her standing on our front porch watching J.P. as he loaded up his truck to leave for a few months. She couldn't run over to him, hug him or tell him that she'll miss him." He paused to quell his emotions. "She couldn't kiss him goodbye. He never even looked over at her. He couldn't. She cried all night, Sara."

"That does sound difficult. It sounds like you do your best, however, to try and show her your support. She has a wonderful brother, Cole. She is very lucky to have you in her life."

"Thanks, Sara. It was helpful to talk about it. But if you don't mind, I think I'm gonna hit the hay."

"Sleep well. Think of me."

"There's never a moment that I don't, beautiful. Good night, Sara Thompkins."

Hanging up the phone that evening Sara felt better than usual at the end of her hectic days. Cole revealed some of himself to her that night. A warm feeling settled in her stomach, knowing that he felt comfortable enough to lean on her for a bit. She liked to think that she helped Cole, even a little. He'd done so much for her.

December 2010

The Beckers traditionally celebrated their Christmas meal in the afternoon. That year the family had a Christmas brunch instead. The change allowed Cole and Sara to celebrate with both families, having dinner later that evening with the Tompkins.

Proudly, Sara stood beside Cole in the Beckers' living room. A bubble of excitement swelled in her chest at the realization that she was standing beside this amazing man because he had chosen her to be his. Gazing up at him, she noted the shape of his chin and the curve of his smile. He was the most handsome man she had ever met, wearing dark jeans and green sweater over a white button down shirt. His arm slid around her waist to rest his hand on her hip as he talked to his brother. While talking with James his thumb rubbed soothingly over her hip. After a moment, Cole looked down at Sara standing beside him and smiled at her. There was such tenderness in his eyes, Sara hoped she would have his admiration forever. Cole gave her a quick kiss and winked at her. He dropped his arm from her waist, put his flute now only half filled with mimosa down and went to the cheese log on a side table by the couch. The one thing Cole liked most about Christmas was the cheese log appetizer. He could just stand next to the platter with the cheese perched in the middle and surrounded by crackers, eating until the firm ball of salty, nutty, tangy goodness was gone. Sara hadn't noticed that one of Cole's family members had occasionally lured Cole away from the platter under the pretense of showing him or telling him something of relative unimportance until his brother James pointed it out to her.

"Otherwise, he'll stand there and eat the darn thing until it's gone. But that's not the problem. It's how it affects him."

"Eww."

"You got it. Eww is right. And he whines something awful through it all."

"Thanks for the warning, James. Good to know."

James nodded as if he had just imparted the most important piece of information and possibly even saved the world by doing so.

James didn't bring anyone to the Becker's traditional Christmas gathering this year. He dated on and off throughout the year but hadn't been involved with anyone special that he wanted to invite home for the holiday.

Cole rested his hand on James' shoulder and stood beside his brother. "You didn't bring anyone to celebrate Christmas with us this year."

"No. I guess I'm between interests at the moment."

"You've had a couple short-term relationships over the past several months, haven't you? There was the leggy blonde. What was her name, Vanilla, or something?"

"Camilla. Yes, earlier this year. We were together for four months. It fizzled after three months, really."

"No one recently, though?"

"My classes this past semester were tough. I didn't do a whole lot of socializing. But not to worry, the semester is over. I'll be back out partying soon. I have to ease my presence back onto the scene slowly, so as not to shock people, you know?"

"So, what you're really saying is no one wanted to spend the holidays with you?" Cole joked, unsure if he just never paid attention enough to notice or if James had actually begun to socialize.

"No, Cole, what I'm saying is I've been a good boy and studying. No time for play."

"I'm sensing you've been giving us all the wrong impression. There's more to you than the quiet and serious James who likes to fuck. You like to really play."

"I do." There was a flicker of a devious smile evident along with his response.

Cole felt a shift in how he's always thought about a brother he believed he knew so well. It wasn't a good or bad feeling. He wanted to know more but now wasn't the time to delve deep. He did want to let James know that he was interested. "So you haven't had time to play, you say?"

James knew his brother wouldn't let it go. "Okay, I play regularly, hard and dirty but not with anyone in particular. So, there was no one special to bring to home for Christmas."

"Well, there's always your favorite angel Christmas ornament. We know that you pine for her, and she'll never let you down, James." Cole was referring to an angel ornament that the Beckers put on their Christmas tree every year. James had mentioned that it was his favorite ornament while decorating the tree with his siblings. And as siblings do, Cole and Audra teased James mercilessly, saying that James secretly desires the angel which the ornament depicts.

"I think you've had too much cheese log." James took the opportunity to walk away from his brother and went to refill his glass of eggnog.

The two hour ride to the Thompkins' farm seemed longer than usual. There was slightly more traffic on the road than usual but also after the Christmas brunch he ate, Cole was feeling a bit sleepy driving. It didn't help that Sara fell asleep almost as soon as they got onto the highway. He managed to stay awake enough to get them to their destination safely.

For the first time since meeting Sara in March, Cole met his girlfriend's mother. Filling her wheelchair and even overflowing a bit, the large woman with graying hair and large round eyeglasses stared back at him. Her skin was sallow looking, her face etched with deep lines. The thin cotton house dress she wore exposed her lower legs and left it possible to see the sores on her purple skin. Their meeting had been as he had expected it would be like. Mrs. Thompkins was sticky-sweet when she spoke to Cole. She was sure to tell him that he was such a nice "boy" and by all her accounts basically had Sara married off to him already. It was uncomfortable, but Cole tolerated it and it was made bearable only by the understanding, sympathetic looks Sara, Beth, and Ricky gave him.

At dinner, she insisted on feeding herself the pureed version of the Christmas dinner Sara and her sister made. The tremor of her hand holding her utensil caused much of the intended mouthful to land in a trail from her plate to her mouth. This included the shelf of her chest, covered with a bib. Cole felt uncomfortable sitting at a table with an adult voluntarily wearing a bib. Much of the time Sara had been timely in wiping her mother's mouth of the puree which didn't made it or leaked from her mother's mouth, but on occasion throughout the meal Cole saw some food clinging to the woman's face. Though he wished that it didn't bother him, the sight was disturbing.

Handfuls of soap bubbles oozed over the edge of the sink onto the countertop as Sara reached in to remove a plate. "Cole seems to be doing okay," Beth said to Sara while they did dishes alone together in the kitchen after dinner.

Sara lifted her eyebrows in a look of disbelief at her sister.

"Well, I mean considering...okay, he looks like he'd bolt out of here so fast and without looking back if given the opportunity."

The sisters laughed at the truth of the situation.

"I'm sorry that it has to be this way for you, Sara. I truly am."

Sara let out a deep sigh. She didn't have anything to say, she felt sorry for herself as well.

"You like him a lot, don't you?" Beth had put the dish that she had been wiping dry down on the counter and faced her sister.

"Yes. A lot. I keep trying to push him away, but he won't leave me alone." Sara tried to smile but it turned into a frown.

"He's a good man. You can't let him go, Sara. It's obvious that you both want to be together."

"I don't want to let him go. It's just the only thing I can do. I can't give him what he wants and needs. I don't know how long my role as mom's caregiver will be for. I can't bring him into this. These are my burdens. I won't do it."

"It won't be forever, Sara. Ricky and I help as much as we can. I think we do okay taking care of mom, don't you?"

How could she tell her sister just how taxing it was caring for their mother if her sister couldn't see it for herself? Beth had a family and house of her own to take care of. She couldn't help take care of their mother as well. "Sure, we do," she said weakly.

"Sara, you'll get married and have all those children that you want so badly. Not just now but it will happen, sweetheart. Your someday will come along."

There it was again, talk of her "someday." She was beginning to believe that there would be no someday for her.

"Someone get me my sweater. It's gosh darn cold in here." Mrs. Thompkins let her needs and desires be known regularly throughout the day and evening, never with a please or a thank you.

"I'll get it." Ricky went to the coat closet in the entryway to fetch the sweater.

He returned to the living room, and as he handed her the sweater, she said, "Do something about the chill in here."

Ricky turned and rolled his eyes at Cole before tending to the fireplace. An almost imperceptible smile crossed Cole's face.

"Cole, come sit next me." Sara's mother patted the armchair alongside her wheelchair.

Really? Do I have to? Cole hoped the ladies would be finished doing the dishes soon so Sara could save him. He moved from the couch to the armchair as requested.

"My Sara is a very good woman." Cold, filmy eyes stared at him. Her face was devoid of expression. She was trying to make a point. Cole went along with her, let her believe she still had some power over her daughter and that she could be threatening to him.

"Yes, that's why I'm drawn to her."

Warm, stale breath made up the sigh she expelled, causing Cole to turn his face away from her momentarily to avoid breathing it in.

"Please, know that I respect your daughter greatly. I admire her and believe her to be a treasure. I hope that you don't spend time worrying about me breaking her heart. I couldn't possibly imagine doing that to her purposefully." Cole was relieved when Mrs. Thompkins' relaxed back in her wheelchair with a soft smile.

Cole stayed as long as he could stand to after dinner, just long enough to not appear ungrateful. But he easily used the excuse of the long drive back home to leave earlier than he intended to that evening. Sara stood from the living room couch, adjusted her skirt and walked Cole to the front door. She handed him his jacket from the coat closet.

"I'm sorry, Cole. It was obvious that you were uncomfortable tonight. I was afraid you might be, but I'm not sure how I could have made it any better. Maybe I should have told you not to come."

"I wish I could have enjoyed myself more, Sara, for your sake. Please don't feel that I don't like your family…"

"I know, Cole. Don't worry. I know how difficult it is to look at her and to even like her at this point. My mother wasn't always this way. But she needs us now. I have to do this."

"I understand."

"Yes, of course you do because you're an amazing person." Sara wrapped her arms around Cole and hugged him close, breathing in his familiar scent of sandalwood and ginger. It permeated the sweater covering his chest she rested her cheek against. She relished the warmth of his body. His hand came up and fingers played with her hair. "That doesn't mean that you have to like it or even put up with it, though. And you know it's the reason I never invite you here. But thank you so much for coming today. It really helped to get her off my back about her never having met you. Now, of course, she'll wonder when the next time is that she's going to see you again, so I probably just opened a big can of worms!"

"I'm very willing to come out again if it will help make your life easier. Just go easy on your expectations of me, okay?"

"Cole, you're the best thing that's happened to me, well, ever." Sara looked at Cole. Her eyes were wet. She closed them tight and turned away from him.

"Hey." He turned her gently back to facing him and hugged her close to his body. He rested his cheek on her head and rubbed a hand along her back to soothe her.

"Talk to me, Sara."

Tears ran down her cheeks. "I'm just confused, Cole. My life is so difficult right now. I don't want to bring that into what we have together. They are my burdens to bear. I don't want you to feel that I'm pushing you away, but I don't know what else to do. It's the only thing that seems to make sense."

"To push me away from you? That seems to make sense to you?"

"Not because of you or anything you've done. Because of me and my burdens."

"I won't be pushed away, Sara, so don't even try, you'll be wasting your time."

"I can't stand the selfish feeling I have keeping you in my life right now."

Cole crashed his mouth to Sara's, effectively quieting her. He pushed his tongue into her mouth and found hers, stroking sensuously along the length of her tongue.

"Feel how much I want you?" He ground his hips against Sara's. "I want to be in your life, Sara. If you wanting to be with me is selfish, then I guess I'm guilty of being selfish as well. All I want is to be with you, any way I can."

Sara took her coat from the closet and put it on. She grabbed Cole's hand and led him out of the house. Cole struggled to put his jacket on as she pulled him by his hand across the lawn and into the barn. She began unbuttoning his jeans. He grabbed her upper arms and walked her backward, pressing her body against the wall with his. She could hear his breathing become deeper and felt his heart beat in his chest. The eyes she looked into were dark, she could see his desire. Sara leaned forward to meet his lips for a heated kiss. Clouds of cool night air, warmed with their passion, rose from their mouths.

"Cole."

He undid the buttons of her blouse and pushed it open, exposing the sheer cream colored bra she wore beneath. The cool air against her skin was a little bit of a shock. Cole grasped a breast and placed it in his mouth. He ran his tongue over and around the hardened nipple still covered by her bra. Sara moaned at the feel of his soft, warm tongue sliding over her erect nipple. She relished the feel of his grasp on her breast, firm and demanding.

"I love your breasts."

"I've noticed."

He smiled at her through hooded eyes.

She tugged the zipper of his jeans down and reached in. His size was much larger than her small hand. She brought the full length of him out. His hands went back to her upper arms, holding her against the wall as his mouth moved to place kisses from her breast, over her collar bone and along her neck. She placed her arms around his neck. He slid his hands down her arms, gathered her skirt around her waist and with his hand under her buttocks, lifted her. She wrapped her legs around his waist. He moved the scrap of silky material between her legs aside and swiped a finger through her folds. He smiled, satisfied at feeling how wet she was. Sara leaned forward and took his bottom lip into her mouth. She gasped against his mouth as he entered her in one hard thrust. He closed his eyes.

"You feel amazing." Then he whispered her name like a prayer.

Sara moved her hips, trying to feel more of him. He pulled back slowly until he was almost out of her, then quickly pushed back in. Her head rolled to one side.

"So good."

Cole developed a steady rhythm, and she met him

with each thrust. Their breathing quickened.

"Harder," she groaned, and he complied. Cole caught a breast with his mouth and sucked hard on her nipple.

"Cole." Her walls tightened around him and her body shuddered. Nails dug into his shoulders. He nipped gently on her neck as he pushed into her hard against the wall. "Fuck, Sara." With great force, he emptied into her.

They held each other for a long moment with her legs still around him and him holding her up. When their breathing had slowed, Sara lowered her legs. Cole helped her to steady herself once her feet were on the ground.

"That was amazing. I don't think I've ever come that hard." He kissed her gently.

"Merry Christmas, Cole!"

He leaned his forehead against hers. "I must have been a very good boy this year."

January 2011

Sara wasn't able to get away from her duties at home on New Year's Eve as she had hoped, so Cole went to a party at the polo club with James. It was a casual party with a cash bar, catered food, and a DJ. James wore the party hat he was provided with when they got to the party as he moved Cole about the room, introducing his brother to his teammates. They stopped and talked to Justin Carver for some time. Justin was in James' class all through school.

"What are you doing these days, Justin?" Cole asked.

"Working on my dad's farm and part-time at the feed store." The Carvers owned a small vegetable farm. They sold most of their produce at Carnegie's Farmer's Market held throughout most of the year on Saturday's in the empty parking lot in town.

"How is old Mr. Duggan?" Cole referred to the older gentleman who owned Carnegie's Feed and Mercantile, also in town.

"Old." They all laughed. "No, he's doing pretty well for his age."

The phone in Cole's pocket vibrated. He excused himself and went into a hallway to read Sara's text.

Sara: *Having fun?*
Cole: *Not as much as if U were here.*
Sara: *U know I wish I were.*
Cole: *I'd only spend the evening kissing U*
Sara: *Sounds good 2 me!*
Cole: *My hands would be all over U*
Sara: *Oooh! Where?*
Cole: *Your sweet ass.*
Sara: *And where else?*
Cole: *I'd stand behind U, arms around U, cock grinding against your ass and brush my fingers under your luscious breasts*
Sara: *Sweet! I'm wet but gotta run. Kisses.*
Cole: *No! I want to hold U a bit longer. Like 4ever.*
Sara: *4ever?*
Cole: *Yes, Sara.*
Sara: *That sounds like strings.*
Cole: *So be it.*
It was a moment before she replied.
Sara: *text U again later.*

Shit. What did I do? I probably scared her off. If this is the kind of stuff I'm texting her now after a few beers, what the hell am I gonna text later tonight? He couldn't shut off his phone. He could say that he hadn't felt his phone vibrate. Cole stepped back into the party and looked for James. After a moment he saw James walking toward him holding two bottles of beer. James held one out for Cole to take.

"Thanks, bro'." Cole took a long draw from the bottle.

"Text?"

"Yeah, sorry."

"No worries. How's it going with Sara?"

"Good and bad. She's awesome, but her mother needing help takes up all of Sara's time."

"Sucks. She seems really nice. You gonna keep seeing her?"

"I can't stop. I'm so addicted to her. It's kinda scary, James."

"Thought this was no strings attached?"

"It was."

"Not anymore?"

"I don't think so."

"Is she okay with that?"

"I don't know but sooner or later I'll find out."

"Good luck, bro'."

"Thanks. Who's got your interest these days?"

"No one in particular."

"Never is." Cole put his hand on his brother's shoulder, and they both smiled. Cole knew if there was anything bothering James or anyone important in his life that James would talk to Cole when he was ready. Cole was just sure to ask every now and again. He was glad to have sobered up enough by midnight that when Sara texted that second time, Cole didn't text anything too crazy or scare Sara off.

March 2011

When it had been a year that he'd known Sara, Cole thought the situation couldn't last much longer. There had been many times when Cole had wanted to throw in the towel on his and Sara's relationship. He kept reminding himself that Sara's life as caregiver to her mother was only temporary. Sara invited Cole to her family's farm for traditional corned beef and cabbage dinner on St. Patrick's Day. Again, she wasn't able to get away to go out with Cole. He wanted to take Sara back to the Irish pub where they met in Greenville one year before. He settled for time with her at her family's home. Sara texted her sister and asked Beth to sit with their mom for an hour after dinner so Sara and Cole could take a walk together. Beth agreed and for that Cole was thankful.

Their walk went only as far as the barn. Sara turned on only minimal lighting and spread a blanket over some hay in empty stall. She sat on the blanket and held her hand out, inviting Cole to join her.

Cole hesitated for a moment. It burned him that this was how he and Sara had to spend time together. Sneaking into the barn and having sex on a bed of uncomfortable hay. It's not what she deserved and just plain not what he wanted for them. But if he wanted to spend time with Sara this was how it had to be. So he lowered himself to sit next to her.

"I know this isn't ideal, Cole. We can just go for a walk like we said we would, if you'd rather."

She knew what he was thinking. They were good together like that.

"You just deserve better, Sara."

"I don't even deserve you, but get over here and kiss me."

He smiled at her. "You deserve great things, Sara. Things I can give you, want to give you but…"

"Let's not think about that, Cole. There's nothing we can do, so let's just enjoy our time together, please."

He gazed into her eyes and brushed his knuckles over

her cheek. "You are so beautiful. Inside and out, Sara. You amaze me, and I feel so lucky to know you."

"Wow, I just feel tired and worn out. It's hard to believe that anyone could think anything like that about me."

"And I don't like that that's how you feel. All I see is your beauty. All I want is to be with you, always."

"What do you mean, Cole?"

"I mean that I want to have you in my life, in some way or another…"

"I don't know what's going to happen, Cole. You can't talk like that."

"I certainly can say what I want. An inconvenient reality doesn't mean I can't hope. And doesn't mean that you can't have hope either."

"An inconvenient reality? Is that what I am, inconvenient?"

"You know that we have an inconvenient reality, Sara. I won't let you give up on hope or try to ruin mine."

"I hate this, Cole! I try to be strong and do what's right." Sara was crying now. She held her face in her hands. "It's been a year. I know she's my mother, but I don't want to do this anymore." Sara couldn't believe what she was saying. Both hands came up to cover her mouth, and she looked like she was in shock. She had never talked like this and certainly would never allow herself to say these things to anyone. Why was she saying this now?

"No, don't have guilt about how you feel. Anyone would be as tired as you are doing what you do day after day. It's only normal. It doesn't mean that you don't love your mother. You are amazing, so strong, Sara. Look at me." He lifted her chin with one finger to look at him. "And as much as you want to push me away because you think it's the best thing to do you know that we're in this together. You're not doing this alone. We've both had our moments of panic when we realized how much we meant to each other. I know that you can't imagine me with another woman or your life without me in it just as I can't imagine you with another man or my life without you in it. That's because we love each other. Yes, Sara, we are in love."

Cole rested his forehead on hers. "Now let me show you what you mean to me." He wiped away the tears on her face with the pads of his thumbs, then kissed her gently on her lips.

A wave of relief came over Sara at being encouraged to allow herself her true feelings. "I love you, too, Cole. You're right, we are in love." She threw her arms around his neck and closed her eyes with a sigh. "So love me, please."

"Yes, ma'am." With a smile on his face, Cole gently leaned Sara back onto the blanket over the hay.

April 2011

That April, Audra celebrated her eighteen birthday. It was a special birthday for her. Cole knew his sister hoped their father would no longer expect J.P. to travel as much for the farm. She hoped she would be viewed and respected as an adult in making her own decisions about her life. Cole and James knew J.P. would be in the middle of a few months of traveling to races on Audra's birthday, so they wanted to do something special for her. They threw her a birthday party, invited all her friends and had all her favorites: pizza, root beer, and birthday cake.

"This sucks that J.P. couldn't be here for your birthday," Mary commiserated.

"It does suck. He sent me a package, though!"

"In the mail? What was it?"

"A blow up birthday cake!"

"With the candles and all? I've seen them in the store. How f-in sweet is that?"

"Yeah, well, my dad didn't think so."

"Oh, Audra, I'm sorry. Has he said anything about when J.P. will be done traveling for the farm?"

"No. Not yet."

"Hopefully he will soon."

"Hopefully."

J.P. was upset about missing Audra's eighteenth birthday. He wished he could have been with her. The best he could do was to send as innocent a present as he could come up with. On the road, Celestra did well through the Spring Race season, though not spectacular. She still needed more training to reach her full potential. She would be J.P.'s focus after Manuel retired in May.

May 2011

The retirement party for Manuel was held outside on the lawn at the guest house. It was a convenient spot for such events since the caterers could use the kitchen and there were bathrooms for guests to use.

Cole was so happy Sara was able to attend the party, even if for just a few hours. With his father having invited all of Manuel's immediate and extended families as well as all of the farm staff present, there were about hundred guests. The skirt of the light pink sundress she wore swirled around her legs as she walked across the lawn toward Cole. When she reached him, she placed her hands on his chest and went up onto her toes to give him a kiss. She smelled like sunshine. Cole couldn't keep his hands off of Sara the whole afternoon. Often throughout the party he lavished her with kisses and always had a hand touching her body. It was difficult, however, knowing that his sister wanted the same opportunity with J.P. but could not.

Cole decided it was a good time to act on a plan he had been working on. Ever since a conversation he and Audra had on the day she got J.P.'s birthday gift in the mail, he planned on giving J.P. a key to the small house. Cole realized then that the couple didn't have many options when it came to being together with Audra still living in their father's house and J.P. living in communal housing. He got Sara a glass of wine from the open bar set up on the lawn and reluctantly asked her to hang out by herself for a short while. Cole went to the main house, into the kitchen drawer and grabbed an extra key for the small house. He had made several extra copies of the house's keys and stored in a kitchen drawer. No one would notice one missing key from the pile. He pocketed the key and went back to the party. He found Sara and checked in with her. She was chatting happily with one of Manuel's cousins and still sipping her wine. So he left her there for a few more minutes and stood by edge of the tented area on the lawn. Finally, he spotted J.P., talking to group of men near the center of the tent. He walked up beside J.P. and asked, "Got a minute?"

"Sure."

"Grab us some beers and meet me beyond the barbeque pits."

A moment later J.P., armed with two beers, stepped into the periphery of the party where he found Cole. Cole took one last sweeping look through the crowd and once he was sure that his father wasn't privy to the two of them talking, he presented J.P. with a key. Cole explained that he had made a copy of the key to the small house for J.P. to keep.

"Nobody is ever out here at the house so it's a nice

little retreat. Sara and I come here from time to time. There are clean sheets on the bed in the master bedroom. The catering company has rights to the kitchen and the downstairs bathroom only, until ten tonight. After that the place is yours. Going forward, seeing as we'll be sharing the place we might need to work out a 'tie on the doorknob' signal or something," Cole joked.

"Cole, this is quite generous of you. Are you sure? I can return the key."

"The key is yours to keep. How else are you two going to work on a relationship? Neither of you can exactly bring the other home for the night. Just be good to her."

"Thank you, Cole." J.P. shook Cole's hand and pocketed the key.

Cole returned to Sara, who now stood near the small house with her phone to her ear. Just as he got to her side she hung up her phone.

"Gotta go?"

"Yeah, I'm sorry, Cole."

Cole shrugged. What else could he say? It was what it was. He walked Sara to her car, kissed her for a long, intimate moment and then asked, as he always did, that she text him when she was home safe.

August 2011

Initially, the rain had been welcome that summer in South Carolina. The months before had been dry. The weather was beginning to affect the growing season for fruits and vegetables at local farms. But when the rain fell hard and for seemingly weeks on end it began to cause new problems.

Bridgeton Pass had fared well overall. The staff

worked hard to keep the horses dry but also allowing outside time followed by meticulous grooming. Their efforts paid off as none of the horses became ill. Leaks eventually surfaced in the barn roof, giving Tanner and some of the hands a run for their money to keep up with repairs.

The Beckers led a fund raiser to aid a local elderly man who lost his house to flooding because of the storms. Since Audra had graduated high school in June, she had plenty of free time and thus led most of the efforts. At about that time, Audra began working temporarily in the office at Bridgeton Pass. While James worked on the final year of his master's program, Audra took over some of James' responsibilities. Cole enjoyed seeing his little sister around the office. One of his new favorite pastimes, since Audra had been in the office, was to set up a mini hunting blind in the hallway and from there shoot spit balls at Audra while she sat at James' desk. Apparently, he found out, he underestimated his sister because she saved up all of the spit balls and at the end of her first month working in the office Cole found them dispersed within his desk drawer.

September 2011

Late in the afternoon one Tuesday, Cole received a call from Sara.

"My mom was admitted to the hospital today."

"Oh, what's wrong?"

"Her blood work is messed up. They have her on some IV meds. It looks like she'll be there for a few days while they try to get everything under control."

"Is she in any pain?"

"No, no more than usual."

"Well, that's good. May I take you out and spoil you?"

"I think that would be okay. Actually, I'd love it."

"How about I drive out there, stay over tonight and work from your house for a few days? We can spend the evenings together when you come home from work."

"That sounds wonderful. Careful driving, and I'll see in a few hours."

"See you in a few hours, Sara."

Sara hung up the phone and did a little happy dance. Then she went about picking up the house before taking a shower. Paying close attention to special areas, she shaved and then applied a fragrant lotion. Using a low setting, she blew her hair dry. When she wrapped herself in her soft terry robe and settled onto the living room couch with a book, she noted that she still had about forty-five minutes before Cole would arrive.

Cole pulled into the driveway at Sara's house and looked at the clock on his dash. It was after nine o'clock. Not bad. A light was on in the living room. After grabbing his overnight bag from the backseat of his car, Cole went up the stairs to the side door of the old farm house. He knocked and then again louder when there was no answer. Cole smiled to himself, thinking she must have fallen asleep waiting for him. He set his bag on the porch, went down the stairs and around the house to a window that looked into the living room. There she was, asleep on the couch. The soft light from the lamp's bulb illuminated her face. Her mouth was closed and set in a gentle, lilting smile. Long, feathery lashes rested on her cheeks. A gap in the opening of her robe revealed creamy skin but only enough to provide a hint of the full breast beneath. The sight before him was angelic. Just then, her lips parted slightly and a hand moved to lie on her stomach. Cole went back to the door and knocked again. Moments later a sleepy Sara came to the door.

"Hey, baby, sorry to wake you." Cole wrapped his arms around her waist and pulled her close. She was warm and smelled delicious.

"Mmmm…I'm so glad you're here."

"You must be pretty tired. Did you spend the whole day at the hospital?"

"Come in." She moved away, allowing Cole to step into the entryway. "Most of the day."

"Can I get you anything, some tea?"

"Oh, Cole, you just drove two hours. Come in for a minute, first! Have a seat in the living room. I'll put on the tea kettle, then join you."

When Sara returned to the living room, Cole was seated on one end of the couch. He motioned for her to sit next to him.

"Put your feet in my lap."

"Are you really going to rub my feet?" she asked with enthusiasm.

The smile he gave her was the one that melted her every time. Sara shimmied into place on the couch, giving her feet over to Cole's talented hands. Grunts, groans, and sighs of relief were interrupted by the whistle of the tea kettle. Sara felt like her whole body was made of jelly. There was no way she was getting up to tend to the tea kettle. Lucky for her, Cole was rather astute.

"I'll get it." He stood and looked down at her resting on the couch. She mouthed a thank you.

Cole went into the kitchen and turned the burner off under the kettle. He pulled one cup down from the cabinet shelf. There was more than a good chance that Sara was going to be asleep again by the time he made it back into the living room with tea. From the tin on the kitchen counter, Cole took a tea bag, placed it in his cup and filled it with water from the kettle. At the entrance into the living room he leaned against the door frame and watched Sara sleep while sipping his tea. *God, she's beautiful. How did I get so damn lucky to have her in my life?* Almost as soon as his heart began to feel full and happy, the realization of what life was like for them came crashing through just as it always did when he began to dream about Sara. He dropped his head and looked into his tea cup. It had grown cold. He went to the kitchen and placed the cup on the counter, then went back into the living room. There, he scooped Sara into his arms and brought her to her bed. She stirred while he fumbled getting her under the sheets but soon was back to being sound asleep. Cole undressed and crawled into her bed beside her. He listened to her steady breathing. How long could he continue to have a relationship with Sara like this? One where her mother's needs come first. He didn't know.

"Not a bad way to wake up." Cole lifted the sheet and smiled at Sara down between his legs.

"Yeah," she said between licks.

"Mmmm." Though he enjoyed the feel of her tongue along the length of him, he gasped when she took him into her mouth. "Yes," Cole hissed and reached down with both hands to hold her head in place. Her lips gripped him. Her mouth was warm. She swirled her tongue around the head, then took the length of him back into her mouth. Cole's hips bucked forward, causing her to take him deeper into her mouth, hitting the back of her throat. "Oh, God, Sara." Holding fast onto her head, he developed a rhythm of thrusts. A low growl came from deep within Cole as he quickly pulled out from her mouth and spilled onto himself.

"Gee, baby, that was fucking fantastic."

"You're welcome."

He pulled her up to lay alongside him and kissed her, a long and gentle kiss. "Are you sure you have to go to work?"

Sara giggled and moved from the bed into the bathroom to get a washcloth for Cole. "Sadly, yes. I've taken so much time off because of my mom, I've only got precious few days left. Unfortunately, I'll probably need them to take care of her."

Cole knew she didn't like her situation any more than he did. He nodded solemnly, put on his jeans and went to the kitchen to make coffee and some breakfast while Sara got ready for work.

A little while later Sara walked into the kitchen but stopped briefly to enjoy the view. One of her favorites. Cole at the stove cooking with only his jeans on. The top button undone, no shirt and bare feet. *Is there any sight more delectable than that?* She thought not.

"What are you smiling about?" Cole turned from the stove, facing Sara with a spatula in hand.

"You, the beautiful view."

"Oh, the view from over here is not so bad either."

Sara took the last few steps toward him, rose up on her toes, and kissed the cook.

"My eggs!" Cole broke from their kiss and turned back to tend to saving their breakfast. He heard Sara giggle behind him.

Mrs. Thompkins spent only one night in the hospital. While at work, Sara had received a call from the hospital informing her that her mother was going to be discharged that afternoon. Once Sara called Cole as he worked from Sara's house and updated him, they agreed he would head back to Bridgeton Pass.

November 2011

"Hey, baby, how was your day?" Cole asked when Sara answered her phone.

"Long."

"Yeah. I would rub your feet if I were there."

"Oh, I so wish you were here. And not just to rub my feet. I miss you."

"I know, baby, I miss you too."

"Beth is coming over tonight to cook dinner while I wash mom's hair. It's always such a chore to wash her hair. But at least I won't have to cook as well."

"That's nice of Beth. I'm glad she's helping tonight."

"I just can't wait for the weekend. This week has seemed like the longest week."

"Oh, speaking of the weekend, Audra and I are going on a day long trail ride on Saturday."

"Great! You've been talking about wanting to plan this with her for a while now. I'm glad you both found a time to do this together."

"Really? You don't mind."

"Stop it, Cole. I know you've wanted to spend time with Audra. No, of course I don't mind."

"You're the best girlfriend." Cole's tone was teasing, but he did really mean it. "This trail is a great ride. It's long and goes far up into the mountains. It's so beautiful up there."

"So, you've been on this trail before?"

"Sure, a number of times. But neither Audra nor I have been up there in some time."

"Well, it sounds like you'll have a great time then."

Cole and Audra believed they would have a great day. The siblings packed their horses for a long trial ride, including lunches, and headed out early Sunday morning. The sun was bright and rose as they traveled beyond the far pasture before heading up into the mountains. Quickly they began catching up with each other. Used to seeing and being around each other so much they were always up to date on what was happening in their lives. Since having met Sara, Cole had spent a bit less time with his sister. Though he saw her in the office now that she was working there temporarily, the farm had been so busy lately that they've rarely had time to talk. So, for each of them this day together was something they had been looking forward to.

Audra anxiously told Cole that J.P. had arranged a time to meet with their father the next day to tell him of her and J.P.'s growing love for each other.

"This is good, Audra. Once J.P. talks to Dad, then you two can move forward." Cole knew she was concerned about what the results of the conversation could mean for her and J.P. Just as he has always been able to, Cole went on to ease his sister's fears. But when Audra asked whether he planned to marry Sara, Cole was shocked to hear his own answer.

"I'm not ready to think about marriage yet, to anyone."

More than likely he said this because he was enjoying his day with his sister so much that he didn't want to ruin it with the pain that went with talking about how much he loved Sara but didn't have a clue whether they had a future together because of her mother.

It was probably his tone that kept Audra from asking any more about it and instead she changed the subject. Eventually, they rode in silence, the trail climbing higher into the mountains and becoming increasingly more difficult to travel. At a clearing they stopped for rest, water and lunch by a campfire before continuing on their journey.

Cole slowed the pace of his horse to allow Audra to lead when the trail became narrower. It had also become a bit steeper in the section of trail. From behind Audra on her horse, he saw her horse's right hindquarter dip as its hoof slipped off the edge of the trail. In a blur, Audra fell from her saddle. There was a thud followed by Audra screaming. He thought it almost unbelievable to see the large branch lodged in his sister's thigh. Her screams of pain were blood curdling and not something Cole would soon forget. Amazingly, he went about pulling the branch from her leg, cleaning the wound with bottled water and applying a tourniquet with little thought about what it was he was actually doing.

The amount of blood was disturbing. Cole knew this injury was bad and that his sister needed serious help. Soon she was unconscious and her body was pale and limp. After tending to Audra, Cole retrieved her horse, tied it to his and hoisted Audra's body up into his mount's saddle with him. Then he began the arduous trip back down the mountain trail. Cole was half in shock and exhausted, thus not thinking clearly. He managed to remember to check his cell phone every now and again for signal. As soon as he was able to get signal he called James but got only his voicemail. So Cole called J.P. and asked him to head up the trail to meet them and help with getting Audra and her horse down the mountain. It felt like forever to Cole when J.P. finally came into view on the trail. They transferred Audra to J.P. on his mount. When J.P. learned that Cole had not yet called for an ambulance they agreed that Cole should make the call and ride ahead of J.P. to meet with the EMTs when they got there. The seriousness of her injury was further brought to light when upon calling for an ambulance they informed him that they would be sending a helicopter to evacuate her quickly, as a life-saving measure.

The next few hours were critical with emergency surgery to save Audra's leg. They were also made tense when William Becker challenged J.P.'s desire to stand vigil at the hospital for Audra. Not wanting to be in the middle between their father and J.P., Cole and James did their best to diffuse the situation and keep J.P. up to date on Audra's condition. If anything good came from the accident it was the bond that Cole and J.P. formed during those days following her accident. Cole felt that he really got to know J.P. on a different level. Though the trainer had been an employee for several years they were not that close. Cole came to learn just how much J.P. loved his sister and what a caring, sincere man he was.

The time spent getting to know J.P. led to Cole's introspective glance at his own feelings about Sara. He loved her. Of that he was sure. He needed and wanted her to be in his life for the rest of time. The fragility of life he witnessed firsthand during his sister's accident confirmed that. Cole knew he needed to spend some time seriously evaluating his life plan at this point.

December 2011

Sick mother or not, Cole loved Sara. They had been together for over a year and a half, and her mother was still in need of her care. Cole decided he obviously wanted Sara to be in his life for the long haul but was tired of waiting. Whether they married then or waited until after that inevitable day of her mother's death, he loved Sara. And he didn't want to wait. By not waiting, he would have Sara is his life, in his bed, every day. But first, he had to ask her. This was exactly what he planned to do until he began to think that Sara may feel too overwhelmed with her current responsibilities to get married and maybe he should wait to ask her. It was driving him crazy thinking about what to do, so he concluded it was time for a drink with Jeff. It took making a deal to buy dinner as well to get

Jeff to agree.

"So, what's this all about, Becker? All you said was that you were having a problem with a woman." Jeff sounded as if he thought he was about to have the world placed on his shoulders.

"A woman? It's about the only woman there is in my life, Sara. And it's not a 'problem'...oh just shut up and listen. You know she takes care of her mother, right?"

"The Ogre? Yeah." Jeff perused the menu while listening to Cole.

"Nice. Well, the Ogre is still around and it's been over a year and a half."

"Okay, are you asking me for my advice on how to kill her off?"

"If only," Cole whispered.

"It's been a year and a half, huh? Wow, time flies," Jeff speculated.

"Yeah, try finding your perfect match, sweet, hot and just barely within reach keeping you blue balled more often than not for a year and a half, then tell me how time flies." Cole took a swig of his beer and placed the mug down onto the table with more force than was necessary.

"So, you want to marry her but the Ogre's still in the picture?"

"Bingo."

"Poison is a fairly undetectable way, isn't it? I mean, I'm a computer programmer, dude, not a chemist. You'll have to ask our friend, Bob, for that kind of info."

"Dammit, Jeff."

"Well, I don't know what to say. Could you just wait and get married when...you know...the mother dies?"

"I'm tired of waiting. And after the scare with Audra, it made me think that I could easily lose Sara to an accident. I don't want to wait anymore. I've been awfully patient. Too patient. I should have walked away a long time ago. Maybe I should just do that now."

"Bullshit. Yes, you have been too patient, but you also had no other choice. Face it, Sara's the one. That's why you haven't walked and why you're not going to. Just ask her to marry you, Cole. You guys can figure out the when and how later. A woman just wants to know it's gonna happen. It's obvious you love her. She's got to know that. Still, she wants the ring, even if there's no date set."

"I don't know. I'm afraid if I try to give her a ring now she's just going to resent me for putting pressure on her."

"Well, just be sure to tell her there's no pressure. That you want her to wear it now and the rest will come someday, when it's the right time." Jeff watched Cole's face while Cole processed his thoughts. "Just do it."

After his talk with Jeff, Cole felt a sense of relief for the first time in a long while. He had a plan and putting it into place made him feel that his relationship with Sara was finally progressing. First, he had to have a talk with his father.

Placing the pad of paper near the stapler, Cole decided his desk was now perfectly organized. He had spent nearly the last half hour of his afternoon organizing his desk. Nerves. Well, there was nothing else to organize and everyone in the Bridgeton Pass offices went home for the day, except Cole and his father, who was waiting for him in the office down the hall.

Standing in his father's office doorway, Cole transferred the light blue silk tie he had removed earlier that afternoon from one hand to the other and back again.

"Come in, Cole."

Cole lowered his large frame into the leather club chair across from his father. It was already dark outside even this early in the evening at this time of the year. A small table lamp lit the corner of his father's office that they sat in. On the same table as the lamp sat a decanter of scotch, one empty rocks glass and another almost empty. Pouring two fingers worth into the empty glass, William then handed it to Cole.

"So what is it that you wanted to discuss, son?"

"I plan to ask Sara to marry me."

"Well, now." William shifted his eyes from Cole's face to stare into his own glass of scotch. "That's a big step. Sara is a wonderful girl. I'm aware of her family, their farm and their current circumstances. What else do we know of Sara?"

"*I know* that I love her…"

"Yes, yes. Of course you do. Has she been married before?"

Cole furrowed his brow at his father. "No."

"Mmmhmm. No children, maybe with a father somewhere?"

"No, Dad!"

The lines on his father's face tightened. "Well, I've checked the Thompkins' out financially…"

"You did not!"

"I did. Cole, be reasonable. Of course, I did. You have nothing to worry about there."

"This is all so touching, Dad." Sarcasm not withheld, he ran a hand through his hair.

"When were you thinking of getting married?"

"Dad, I wanted to talk to you about…me…and getting married."

"We are."

Cole let out a large sigh in frustration.

William sat up straighter in his chair. "You want to talk about marriage."

"Yes."

"You have loved her for some time now. Do you have doubts?"

"I don't know, Dad. I do love her. I can't image life without her but...this situation with her mother." Cole shook his head slowly from side-to-side, staring off into an empty corner of his father's office.

"Her devotion to her mother certainly is...strong."

"Sara does love her mother. All of the memories I have of caring for Mom while she was sick keep me from being too upset about how much the woman depends on Sara. It's hard to watch Sara live her life this way but worse is the fact that it's been this way for her for so long. And how much longer will this be the way things are for Sara?"

"I see."

"I've tried to consider walking away, but I just can't."

"Because you would feel guilty about leaving her to her situation or because you can't leave her?"

"Because I can't leave her. I want her, Dad. Forever." He let out another large sigh. "I just don't want this to be the way life is for her, for us. Does that make me a selfish bastard?"

"No, son. It makes you human, a man in love. Hers is not a life anyone would want." William hesitated before asking, "Does the family have any idea how...long..."

"No. She keeps holding on. They keep thinking she's on the edge of death, and she keeps holding on."

"Oh."

"As you may be able to imagine, I'm tired of waiting and being patient. That makes me sound like a heartless monster. And then there's the fact that Audra's accident made me think of how I could lose Sara. Those thoughts made me want to just run to the nearest Justice of the Peace with her. Then reality set in. I think about where would we live and how much additional stress being married would add to Sara's life." Cole took a generous sip of his scotch before continuing. "I talked with my friend, Jeff, about all this. He thinks I should just propose and let her know that there's no rush to decide the details of a wedding. He thinks she'll just want to have the ring and know that we will get married when the time is right."

"Your friend, Jeff, seems like a smart guy. I think his suggestions are good ones. What do you think, Cole? You know Sara best."

"I think if I make it clear that there's no pressure behind giving her a ring that she would be happy to be asked to get married. But what if she says 'no?' I couldn't live with that."

"Well, that's certainly a possibility for any couple, Cole. You can't dwell on that thought. That can't be the reason that you won't ask her. I think you do want to ask her and you feel that it's the right time to propose so long as you let her know that there is no pressure." After a moment, William added, "The situation with Sara's mother is unfortunate. It doesn't have to be a barrier to you getting engaged or even married. I'm sure you both support each other. Plus, you know that when Sara's mother finds her peace so will the two of you in your life together. That's what's important to focus on."

"Thanks, Dad. Now about all this other stuff, the business end of my getting married." The two spoke a while longer, sitting in William's office by the light of the table lamp.

After the rush of Christmas was over, Cole began thinking about getting an engagement ring for Sara. Since he hadn't been spending as much time with his sister as he had in the past and J.P. was away overnight at an auction, he decided to recruit her help in the task.

Audra welcomed the knock on her bedroom door. She was bored with reviewing the race horse licensing rules books her father expected her to be familiar with now that she was working for him while James finished his master's program. She felt the dreariness of a rainy Saturday only helped to make the task that much more difficult. "Come in," she hollered, not moving from the bean bag chair where she sat.

Cole entered. "Hey, sunshine."

"What's up?" Audra asked.

"Any chance that you would like to come ring shopping with me this afternoon? Sara called to say her mother needed her, so we canceled our plans to get together today. I thought I'd take the unexpected opportunity to go shop for Sara's engagement ring."

"Really? That's so exciting, Cole!" Her demeanor changed momentarily, becoming more serious. "I mean, I'm sorry to hear that Sara's mom needed her assistance today but...yes! Let's go!" Audra couldn't leave the rules books behind fast enough.

"Are you sure? Looks like you were studying, Audra," Cole said cautiously.

Audra shot her brother a 'whatever' look, grabbed her jacket and left Cole standing in her room.

At the jeweler's shop in town, Audra looked through every case they had. "They are all so pretty, Cole. How will you decide?"

"Gee, that's why I brought you! Don't tell me you can't decide either."

"Well, let's think about what style of jewelry Sara wears," Audra began.

"I don't think I've ever seen her wearing a ring." Cole thought.

"Of course, how about that square blue ring she wore at Christmas?"

With the help of the shop's jeweler, they learned that Sara most likely had worn a princess cut sapphire ring. He showed them some of the princess cut diamonds that he had in various settings. Then explained the basic information a buyer should know when buying a diamond. "What type of metal do you want for the band?" At the questioning looks that Audra and her brother passed between each other the jeweler asked more simply, "Silver or gold?"

Within the next hour Cole had made his choice and purchased a lovely princess cut diamond engagement ring for Sara. Audra had no problem trying the rings on to assist her brother in his selection.

"That was fun!" Audra said, full of exuberance as they walked back to Cole's car from the jewelry shop.

"It was, wasn't it? Thanks for your help, Audra."

"When are you going to give it to her?"

"I'm not sure. Soon." Cole looked pensively off into the distance.

"I think it's romantic. I wish I could be there when you give it to her!"

Cole rolled his eyes. "No way! What if she says 'no?' How embarrassing."

"Sara is not going say 'no!' Cole, really." Audra was exasperated with her brother.

On Thursday that week Cole arrived at his desk after putting a yogurt in the fridge and making a cup of coffee. He paused for a moment uncertain whether he heard loud voices. Listening carefully, he heard what sounded like his father speaking with J.P. A moment later, the door to his father's office opened, and J.P. exited while chuckling. Odd, Cole thought and followed J.P. to the office kitchen. At the same time, James joined them. Pouring a cup of coffee, J.P. looked back over his shoulder at the brothers.

"What's up, guys?"

"I think that's what we're wondering." Cole looked at James, who nodded in agreement.

"You mean what were your dad and I talking about?"

The brothers nodded in unison.

J.P. turned to face them, stirring his coffee. "Well, you know that I just came back from an overnight road trip to an auction, right?

"Yeah, with Eddie and Tommy," James said.

"Right, well, Eddie almost immediately went off to get shit-faced. I looked around for him for a bit, found him with some skank of a woman and just about left him there when he lazed about getting into the truck when it was time to leave."

"Dumb fuck," James said in disgust.

"Yeah, he passed out in the backseat and barfed all over it. Made for a long ride home."

"You're kidding?" Cole asked.

"I wish I was."

"So, he didn't help at all?" James asked.

"No, but Tommy proved to be quite a help. I was glad he came along. That kid's got talent."

Cole pointed at J.P. in emphasis. "I thought maybe he did. He's pretty astute. He's a good worker, isn't he?"

"Yes. His personality and willingness to learn make me think I'm going to work with him on obtaining his Trainer Assistant certification, if he's interested."

The brothers raised their eyebrows at each other. J.P. was thinking ahead.

"That sounds like a good plan, J.P.," Cole said.

"I'll have to talk with your father about it, of course. So, what went on around here while I was away?"

"Nothing," Cole and James said at the same time, making all of them laugh.

January 2012

Cole then put a good amount of thought into when, where, and how he would propose to Sara. He thought about doing it at the Irish pub where they met in Greenville. He also considered the small house at Bridgeton Pass Farm, where he hoped they would live. But in the end, he decided on asking Sara to take a walk with him out to the pastures on her family's farm one crisp evening, as the sun painted cool colors across the sky.

"It's beautiful, isn't it, Cole?" Sara looked out across the span of the horizon on the edge of the pasture. The deep yellow of the setting sun reflected on her face.

"I've never seen anything more beautiful." He hadn't taken his eyes off of her.

Sara turned her gaze to him and smiled. She rose up onto her toes to press her lips to his. "I love you, Cole."

He slid the back of his hand gently across her cheek. Her skin was soft. A light breeze carried wisps of her hair with it and away from her face. "You are everything to me." He wrapped his arms around her waist and pulled her close. "I love you more than anything. I love your smile. I love your heart. I love your laugh. Everything about you. And I never want to live without you." Cole released his hold on Sara, reached into the pocket of his jacket, and brought out the black velvet jewelry box. He opened the lid for her to see the ring he was offering her. "Please, Sara, will you be my wife?"

Sara looked from the ring to Cole and back with what looked like a combination of fear, sadness, and anxiety. "I…I…um…"

Instantaneously, his body stiffened. Cole's fear that Sara would not say 'yes' seemed to be coming true. He closed the lid of the jewelry box but could make himself move no further.

"Cole, I love you but…" She lifted her arms and looked around at the farm surrounding them. "I can't give you what you deserve."

"Not right now, Sara. But someday. Someday, Sara.

Tell me that you'll wear my ring and someday we can be married."

Her twisted expression reflected the torment in her heart. "I want that. I want to be married to you. It's just…I have to say no." Tears fell. Sara covered her face with her hands and ran back to the house.

He closed his eyes and tilted his face toward the sky, still clasping the jewelry box in his hand. It was a possibility that she'd say "no". He knew that, but he had hoped if he let her know that they didn't have to get married right away she would say "yes". He just didn't think his heart could take any more pain. After a long moment he went to the house. Sara was sitting on the couch in the living room with both knees bent, hugging her legs to herself.

"Don't cry, Sara. A marriage proposal is a happy thing, baby. Especially because we know we love each other. Please think about it." He just couldn't understand why there had to be so much pain in their loving each other.

"Please, Cole. I need to be alone right now," Sara said between sobs.

Alone? No, he decided, he couldn't take any more hurt and difficulty loving a woman. "Fine," he said softly and left.

Cole drove back to Carnegie, seething with anger the whole way. Why? Why, did her mother have to come between them over and over again? Dammit, why didn't Sara just take the ring? She even said she wanted for them to be married. Couldn't she have just taken the ring? Didn't she realize how her rejection made him feel?

Sara sobbed as quietly as she could so her mother wouldn't hear. If her mother found out why she was crying it would make her mother feel guilty for needing Sara to care for her. She couldn't, wouldn't, do that to her mother.

It was Sara's duty to care for her mother and that included making her mother as comfortable and happy as possible in her final days. But she hadn't been able to stop her sobs. Eventually, Sara called her sister, desiring someone who would understand to just be with her for a little bit. On hearing what Sara had told her, Beth came to the family's house to comfort her sister.

"First, tell me you didn't say no to Cole's marriage proposal." Her sister's tone had a bit of a bite to it.

"Beth, you're supposed to make me feel better! I had to say no."

Her sister took in a deep breath of air. "Sara, you can't stop living your life."

Sara's blue eyes were staring up at her sister, who stood over her with her arms crossed. Beth sat beside Sara on the couch.

"I know this hasn't been easy for you. I'm sorry you've had to make all the changes in your life that you have and to take on most of this burden. But because of that you have to keep living as much of your life as normally as possible. So when a gorgeous hunk of a sweet, loving guy asks you to marry him, you say yes."

"Beth, how can you say this to me? You know what my days are like. You know I can't give him or a relationship between us what it deserves. And I can't live like that. If I'm going to commit myself to someone it has be when I can do just that, commit."

"You are doing a great job…" Beth began.

"I'm not fishing for compliments or trying to make you feel guilty…"

"Sara, listen to me! You are doing a great job here caring for Mom, but you have the right to live your life."

"And she has the right to continue to live out hers," Sara countered.

"I swear if you don't call that man and tell him you

will marry him, I'll do it myself. I'll get that ring from him and shove it on your finger. Dammit, Sara, he loves you. That doesn't happen every day. Now, I know you love him. So take the ring. You don't have to get married tomorrow or make it a big thing. Those are details and they can be figured out between the two of you later."

Sara began to cry again. What had she done? She let a wonderful man who loved her, despite all the crap in her life, who wanted to be with her walk out the door. Oh, God, how could she have been so stupid?

"Call him, now."

When Sara didn't react, Beth repeated her directive.

"Okay, I'll call him. Thanks, Beth."

"There you go. That's the sister I know. Go get him, Sara!" Beth gave her sister a kiss on her tear stained cheek. "Call me again if you need me," she said as she left the family's house to return to her own.

Sara washed her face in the bathroom with cool water, trying to collect herself before calling Cole.

"Sara," her mother called as loudly as she could from her room upstairs. Sara had hardly heard her mother's weak voice.

"Coming, Mama," Sara said and went up to her mother's room.

"Sara, sweetheart, sit here a minute." Her mother patted a spot beside her on her bed.

Sara sat on the worn quilt covering her mother's bed. When she expected it to be warm it had actually been cool. Her mother's gray hair was wiry, held together into the bun Sara had made on her head earlier that morning.

"Sara, did that sweet boy, Cole, ask you to marry him? I'm sorry, but I heard you and Beth talking just now."

"Yes, Mama, he did." Sara fought to keep her tears at bay.

"You are going to tell him that you will marry him, aren't you? Beth was right, dear, you can't let real love slip away from you."

"I'm going to call him right now. I'm going to tell him that I do want to marry him." She smiled at her mother.

"Good. I'd love to know that you're happy and married before I leave this Earth. So, don't you dare put off any wedding because of me. I won't be able to attend whether I'm here or in Heaven so there's no use putting off the opportunity for you both to be together."

"Oh, Mama..." Sara hugged her mother's shoulders.

"No, don't you cry anymore. Just go call that boy and do it now."

"Thank you, Mama." This was what Sara really needed, to know she had her mother's blessing before saying "yes" to Cole.

Sara's hands shook as she held the phone, trying to dial Cole's number. He was almost half way back to Carnegie when Sara called.

"Cole, I was stupid to say that I couldn't accept your ring. I'm sorry. Could you find it in your heart to give me another chance, to ask me again?"

Cole's heart nearly jumped out of his chest. "Hold tight, beautiful. I'm turning my car around right now and on my way back to put that ring on your finger."

Sara had never been so happy. She ran up the stairs to her mother and told her that Cole was on his way back to put the ring on her finger. Her mother held her frail arms out as high as she could to summon her daughter for a hug. Sara, in her excitement, bounced gently on the edge of her mother's bed as they hugged. While Sara waited for Cole to return, she called Beth and told her sister the good news.

When he rang the doorbell an hour later, Sara opened the door and began to cry again. Neither said a word. He held Sara tightly and buried his face in her hair. He produced the jewelry box from his pocket again, took the ring from the satin lining and placed it on Sara's hand. Amidst Sara's tears, Cole kissed her like a starving man, feasting on her lips.

"You have made me the happiest man. I love you so much, Sara."

"I'm so happy too. I'm so excited I'm going to be your wife."

Sara was sure to tell Cole that her mother gave them her blessing to not wait to have their wedding. Cole flinched inwardly at learning this information as it reminded him of his and Jeff's recent conversation over dinner and drinks in which they referred to Sara's mother as the Ogre. It was the best thing her mother had ever done for him.

February 2012

Audra's thigh wound had healed well enough that she could return to riding. It was agreed she wouldn't ride alone, at least for the first few times out, to be sure she had the strength and stamina to ride safely. Mostly Cole accompanied her. It was an opportunity to catch up some more with his sister. Just before her accident, Audra and J.P., whom her father had advised against dating, had wrestled with approaching her father to inform him of their relationship. Cole knew that the discussion did happen once things calmed down again after the accident. As far as Cole knew, the talk had gone well. He asked Audra about it.

"Dad's been okay about us. We're discreet, so we give him nothing to complain about."

"Really? He hasn't been smothering you, following you around?"

"No. He really hasn't." After a moment, she added, "Did you know Tanner has been seeing my nurse, Casey?"

"No." Cole laughed. "He has? That's great. I've never known him to have a girlfriend. Dates, but never anything meaningful."

"Yeah, well, they've only been for coffee and a hike so far."

"We'll have to see how it goes!"

"I'm glad you suggested a ride today, Cole. I hate to be the one always asking. I feel like the pestering little sister," Audra said with a smirk.

They took a trail that crossed a large open pasture. The view while riding through that pasture was spectacular. The mountains loomed up along one side, dark, nearly all rock and sparse of new growth. The tall pines rose up from the forest along another side. Though dark, the trees still boasted some green color. The sun had just risen as they were heading out. It hadn't climbed high enough yet, though to burn off all of the fog that hung through the pasture and up along the edge of the tree line.

"I've really wanted to ride with you. I know I've been spending a lot of time with Sara. She knows my family is important to me, though. It's nice that she respects that we each want to have some time with family and friends."

"I like Sara, Cole. She's not fake. And she's pretty. I'm especially glad to know she makes you happy. So, you gave Sara her ring and she loved it, right!"

Cole nodded, smiled and left it at that.

"When do you think you'll have the wedding?"

"We're planning the wedding for next summer. I'd like to have it here, at the farm."

"Oh, that would be so nice! You're such a romantic, Cole."

"Well, it's the compromise I'm hoping to offer Sara." Cole paused. Audra's smile faded. "You know that her father passed away several years ago and Sara's mom isn't capable of living alone. Well, her mother also doesn't want to move from their farm. So, Sara wants to live close to her mother. The compromise would be to have the wedding here."

Audra knew this meant they would live almost two hours away. She was devastated. She'd never been away from her brother. She knew she'd get used to it but that didn't mean that she'd have to like it.

"Well, your home will be a place I can go to and visit." She tried to sound understanding. She knew it wasn't her brother's preference to live so far away.

"I'm hoping that someday we can live here." There was a hint of sadness in Cole's voice.

It was around ten at night by the time Cole pulled in and parked in the driveway at Bridgeton Pass Farms. He had spent the last two nights in a hotel in Greenville and the day in meetings. Grabbing his leather overnight bag from the backseat of his car, he then lumbered up the porch stairs and into the house. In the foyer, Cole dropped his bag and removed his coat. He didn't bother putting the light on in the coat closet, he just reached in and grabbed a hanger, slid it into the shoulders of his tweed overcoat, hung it and shut the closet door. Limited sleep, boring meetings and long drives had left Cole utterly exhausted upon his return.

The kitchen light was on, and he could hear James inside humming to himself, probably fixing a cup tea. It sounded good to Cole, the tea not James' humming, so he went in.

"Hey, big brother. Ooh-wee, did you miss some action today." James looked at Cole, shaking his head slowly and repeatedly dipping his teabag in the cup.

"What happened?"

"Fight. Big fight—between J.P. and Eddie."

"What do you mean?" Cole couldn't believe what he was hearing.

"Well, apparently, when Audra went into the barn this afternoon Eddie welcomed her back after recuperating from the accident. Apparently he missed seeing her around in the barn."

"What did he do? I'll kill that mother—"

James held his hand up to stop Cole from making any further threats. "Well, his hand barely made contact with Audra's butt before J.P. had him on the ground and beat the shit out of him."

"Oh, man." Cole ran his hand over his weary face.

"Yeah, Tanner fired Eddie right there on the spot. He was pretty beat up. J.P. really did a number on him."

"Is J.P. okay? Audra must be a wreck."

"J.P.'s got a broken hand and a bunch of cuts and bruises. Audra's out cold, she took one of the pills that make her sleepy. Dad's not too happy, of course."

"Not happy with J.P.?"

"Yeah, Dad's worried about the farm's reputation. Not sure if Eddie's gonna press charges against J.P. or what might happen."

"I hope Dad didn't give J.P. too much shit. I mean, the guy was defending his daughter."

James just shrugged. "I just hope Eddie lays low and slithers out of sight for good."

"Yeah, really, he could cause some big trouble. Damn that idiot fool."

A long time employee of the farm, Eddie had felt that he had been wronged when J.P. Ryan was offered the trainer apprenticeship seven years prior. Eddie had already been working for the Beckers for several years and had been considered for the position, but J.P., the foreman's cousin at that, had been offered the position. Over the years since J.P. had been hired, Eddie's jealousy had grown. His snide comments had now become harmful acts as J.P. became successful in the position. Eddie had the potential to become malicious, especially after having been fired a few weeks into the new year.

March 2012

On a Tuesday night in the middle of March, Cole prepared to leave his office. The charity organization which the family was involved in was having a dinner tonight, so he didn't want to stay late in the office. Cole's phone rang at five o'clock. Thinking he almost made it out of his office for the day before any disruptions that might keep him later than he hoped, he prepared to hide his annoyance from his voice. As he reached for the phone he saw that it was James calling.

"Let me guess, you're going to be late."

"Yeah, stuck in traffic."

"You mean you didn't make sure to leave on time and you're calling me so you don't have to talk to Dad directly."

"You know me too well. Thanks, Cole. I'll meet you guys at the dinner."

Cole smiled. "All right then, see you there."

Cole thought of ways that James could make it up to him for leaving him to listen to their father complain about James' irresponsibility for being late.

"Did he say when he might get here?"

"Uh, he was in traffic. I think it was hard for him to be able to say when he'd be here."

"Was he going home first? Or coming straight here from Greenville?"

"I don't know…"

"Hold on." William held his hand up to quiet his son.

He pulled his phone from the inner pocket of his suit jacket. Immediately, he stood from his place at the table. With the phone still to his ear, he tugged on the sleeve of Cole's suit jacket.

"We're on our way." He ended the call and stuffed the phone back inside his suit jacket pocket. As he walked away from the table with Cole in tow, he said, "Barn's on fire." The two began to run toward the valet stand.

Initially in shock, father and son rode to their farm in silence for some time, adrenaline thick in the air inside the car.

"How? What did James say?"

"Not much. He just told me it's on fire. I didn't wait for any more information."

"What do you think? It's not dry enough for the hay to be a concern."

"I don't know, Cole. I just hope it wasn't set. I'm more concerned about what will be left when we get there."

His father's thoughts came as a shock. "You think someone might have set the barn on fire?"

"I don't know, Cole. I wouldn't put it past Eddie Fisher to do something this malicious."

"Oh my God! To ruin our chances at the Spring Races."

"Could be what he wants."

"He wouldn't hurt the horses, would he?"

July 2012

Negotiations to have Miles Carney, a top jockey, ride Jericho in the upcoming spring race season were underway. The buzz business like this caused was what Cole liked best about his job. And his buzz only got bigger when his father informed him that he had been contacted by Myrna Bingham, owner of Watchover Farms, with a proposal to breed her championship mare with Jericho. Miss Bingham's farm was one of the biggest, most successful race horse farms. A deal like this would be huge, and Cole got hard just thinking about working on the negotiations. Bridgeton Farms was climbing its way back from the devastation it suffered following the barn fire in March.

Though there was no proof Eddie was involved with the barn fire, the fire caused significant costly damage and took the life of the farm's potential championship horse, Celestra. Eddie's involvement was confirmed, however, when a hired thug attempted to kill the farm's next potential championship horse, Jericho, harming Audra in the process.

It had been a pretty good day. Audra put together a graduation party for James, who finished his master's degree. The best thing about the party, in Cole's opinion, was the cheese log appetizer. He was in heaven. Sara was only marginally successful in her attempts to keep him from the tray. Observing the party from the periphery, Cole thought it was interesting to watch James interact with his group of friends. They mostly seemed to be boring intellectual types. These people appeared to be odd choices for friends when juxtaposed to the playboy, party side that Cole knew of his brother. And then there was Elena. There was something about her. She just didn't fit into the picture well. And this was what he meant when his father asked him and J.P. their opinion on James' girlfriend. He was mildly shocked when J.P. suggested that James may be gay.

Following the party, Cole and Sara retired to the small house. Knowing that it would be late by the time the party was over, Sara arranged for her sister to stay overnight with their mother. Sara would drive back home in the morning. Cole couldn't help but look around the house and wish it could be his and Sara's house. The wedding was coming up soon with most all of the preparations done so he and Sara would get to enjoy a rare quiet Saturday night alone. The night didn't turn out to be quiet, however.

Cole froze in place, lying next to Sara in bed. Something was wrong. He heard sirens off in the distance. This far out from the downtown, if sirens could be heard at Bridgeton Pass Farms, then the farm was the only place they could be heading to. He felt Sara's delicate hands on his chest. They were still when moments earlier they had been roaming over his body.

"Oh my God, Cole, sirens." She had heard them too.

They raced from the bed, dressed quickly and went outside. Cole panicked to see Audra being placed on a stretcher to be put into an ambulance. He watched the EMTs attempt to arouse her while wheeling the stretcher to the open doors of the ambulance. Cole stood helpless, searching for answers, then went to find Tanner.

"What's going on?"

"Someone was in the barn. Whoever it was got a set of reins around Audra's neck, she passed out. J.P. took off after the guy. The police were right behind J.P. I think they're cuffing the guy now."

Cole went into the barn and found Tommy looking Jericho over. There was a large scratch evident across the horse's thigh.

"Call Doc Waterman," he instructed Tommy. Then asked, "You haven't touched Jericho, have you?"

"No. I've touched nothing, sir."

"Good." Looking around, he saw nothing out of place, then checked each of the other horses. As he suspected, it appeared that only Jericho had been touched. Jericho had been the target, Cole surmised.

Coming from the barn, he saw the police putting the thug into the back of the police car. J.P. and Tanner stood nearby observing.

"Looks like he only touched Jericho. From what I saw, he has a scratch across his thigh. The others horses look fine, nothing seems out of place. Tommy's calling Doc Waterman to come check out Jericho."

They were then joined by William and James, who came from the main house, and then by the officers.

"We searched him and found a syringe on him." One of the officers held up a clear plastic bag with a large syringe inside. "No I.D., though, and he isn't talking."

"Doc Waterman's on his way," Tommy said as he jogged toward the group.

"Good. We'll take some statements and photos for evidence while we wait for Doc Waterman to examine Jericho and report his findings."

The veterinarian was at Bridgeton Pass Farms only a few minutes later. After examining Jericho, Doc Waterman gave his report.

"It appears Jericho suffered only a superficial scratch from the needle of the syringe. I don't think it will scar. I cleaned and dressed the wound. I'll be by again tomorrow to check it. Looking at the syringe that the police confiscated from the guy I can tell that the contents were never dispensed."

"If it leaves a scar could it result in an infraction or disqualification from racing? I mean, given where it's located the officials may think we are just trying to cover something up."

"Well, we have the police here to vouch for you and photos of the fresh wound. I'll be making a full report and statement as well. I don't think you'll have a problem."

With that the police left to lock up the thug. Doc Waterman gratefully accepted a drink of scotch from

William. He followed William and James into the main house.

Audra was kept overnight for observation at the hospital and returned the next day. Though severe, she luckily only suffered soreness and bruises. At James' graduation party the previous day, William informed J.P. that he would be doing much less travel from now on. The couple had been waiting for William to give them this news before they would consider marriage since they planned on starting a family right away. Neither wanted J.P. to be a part-time parent because he traveled for work. They were engaged the next day, after Audra came home from the hospital.

"Would you marry me on Friday?" J.P. was serious, and he wanted to know Audra's answer. "There is an inn up in the mountains that I'd like to take us to for a long weekend away. We could have a small ceremony there on a Friday, just family. Then stay the rest of the weekend for a mini honeymoon."

"That sounds perfect." She truly was excited with the plan.

"Would you feel cheated out of a big wedding, though? I would do a big wedding if that's been your dream," J.P offered.

"I've never dreamed of a big wedding, maybe because my mother wouldn't be there to help me with my gown and fix up my hair. Since I've been helping Sara with her wedding preparations, it all just seems to be such a hassle. No, I'm certain I don't want a big wedding!" Audra and J.P. laughed. "Do you think we could get everything we need together to be able to be married on Friday?"

"I think so. I've checked into what some of the requirements are. Why don't you talk to your dad? I want to be sure he's okay with his only daughter not having a big wedding."

"Sure. Sounds like a good plan!"

Audra brought a pot of tea, two cups and some cookies on a tray out to the living room. She set the tray on the coffee table and began to pour the tea for her and her father.

"Is this an attempt to prove your domestic skills?" William teased. Audra shot back a look relaying that she was not amused, and then smiled. She handed her father a cup of tea and sat next to him on the couch with her cup. "I'm getting married, Dad." She beamed at her father.

"I'm so very happy for you, Audra. You knew all along that the two of you were meant to be. I can honestly say that I am proud of how you both have handled your 'courtship' for lack of better word."

"Thank you."

"He has adored you for a long time. And you, him."

"Are you truly happy for me, Dad? I need to know."

"Yes, Audra. I am truly happy that it is J.P. that you will marry. I know he is a good man and that he loves and adores you. I won't have to worry. I know he will take good care of my daughter." It was exactly what she needed to hear her father say. "You're going to be a beautiful bride," he added.

Audra told her father that she and J.P. were not planning a big, elaborate wedding. She mentioned that they wanted a simple ceremony with a small gathering of family. She was surprised when her father was supportive of their plan.

"So, I'm not squashing a dream you may have had for me to have a big wedding?"

"No, Audra. I want you to have the wedding that suits you."

She told her father of the idea to have it at an inn in the mountains that J.P. had suggested. William really liked the idea. He thought it sounded very romantic. He wasn't surprised when Audra said that they thought their wedding would probably happen fairly soon.

"I'd like for you to live in the small house," William said.

"Wow. That's incredibly generous, Dad. I, we, would love that. Are you sure?" Audra's emotions were somersaulting.

"If you think you will be happy there, I'd like nothing more than to have my daughter and her family here with me at Bridgeton Pass. Please, if you think you will be happy there."

"Yes, yes. I…thank you, Dad." She was crying happy tears as she hugged her father. She thought of her children running across the lawn, playing in the woods behind the house, but best of all that they would be easily able to walk over to grandpa's house and visit. She chuckled a small bubble of happiness out loud.

"What is it?" her father asked.

"I hope that you realize you'll have no privacy with grandkids living next door. I am just imagining them running over to grandpa's house on a regular basis, no matter how much I try to tell them to let you be." She laughed.

"Don't you dare try to keep them from coming over whenever they want to!" He leaned over and kissed Audra's cheek.

Audra and J.P. managed to arrange having their wedding that Friday. J.P. had arranged for a Justice of the Peace to perform the ceremony at the inn and assured that they would have their marriage license that day. Audra worked with the innkeepers to arrange a small meal to be served after the ceremony. They also managed to move their things into the small house as well as stock it with basic foods and household items.

The inn was a large former estate in the Smokey

Mountains. There were flower beds and an herb garden amongst the landscaping. The lawn was large, enough room to hold the ceremony and to accommodate seating for Audra and J.P.'s guests. Audra and J.P. arrived in the morning to settle into their room and enjoy a glass of champagne together before the guests arrived.

The innkeepers, Nadia and Clement, were a pleasant, older couple. Clement showed Audra and J.P. to their room and handed J.P. their room key. The champagne was chilling in an ice bucket on a small round table set in front of a large window that overlooked the back lawn. From that window they saw that the chairs had been set up for the ceremony already. On the patio, two large tables had been set up with chairs for the meal. Audra could see that Nadia had tied ribbons around springs of herbs and placed them in the middle of each place setting. A vase in the center of each table held bunches of wild flowers presumably from the flower beds on the property. "It's beautiful, J.P. What a lovely place to have our wedding." J.P. had opened the champagne and was pouring a glass for each of them. Audra sat at the small table, J.P. pulled his chair closer to hers and handed her a glass of champagne. They clinked their glasses, kissed and sipped champagne. J.P. relaxed in his chair, staring at Audra, unable to take his eyes off of her. She smiled at him. He scooped her up from her chair and brought her to the bed. "Just lie with me here for a bit," he said. He propped himself up on one elbow and traced the edge of her face with his finger. Slipping his fingers through her hair, he admired her sheer beauty. He pulled the strap of her tank top off her shoulder to kiss the bare skin underneath. When he lifted his head to look at her again, he said, "I do." Audra smiled up at him. Then there was a knock on their door. It was Nadia wanting to let them know that some guests had begun to arrive and to discuss some last minute details with Audra.

When Nadia left, Audra went to her suitcase and began to get ready. The Justice of the Peace was scheduled to marry them in an hour. By the window, J.P. stood pushing the curtain aside to peer at the activity.

"Nadia and Clement are setting out crackers and cheese. Looks like they have a bowl of punch and are offering beverages to the guests who have arrived."

"Oh, who has arrived?"

"Your father and James."

Having changed into her sundress, Audra went into the bathroom to prepare. She swiped some blush onto her cheeks, sprayed on some perfume and pulled her hair up into a twist on her head. J.P. walked into the bathroom, stood behind Audra with his hands in his pocket and watched her in the mirror as she applied a bit of lip gloss. He stepped forward, then grasped a few wisps of her hair and let them fall romantically around her face.

"You're not supposed to see the bride before the wedding," Audra teased.

"I'm sorry you're missing out on having your mom here with you on your wedding day."

"Thanks. And I'm sorry you're missing out as well." They held each other's sad gaze for a moment. Audra turned to J.P. and displayed his mother's ring for him. He picked up her hand and kissed it. "You look beautiful," he told Audra. There was another knock on the door and this time J.P. answered it. Sara stood in the hallway. She told J.P. that Nadia had sent her up to their room with flowers for Audra to carry. He let Sara in and went to get ready while the girls chatted.

"You are a lovely bride!" Sara looked like she was going to burst. She handed Audra the bouquet of wildflowers held together with a satin ribbon.

"Thank you, Sara. I'm so glad you're here." She

grabbed Sara's hand and squeezed it gently.

"You're going to be Mrs. Ryan in...mere moments!" Sara could hardly contain herself.

Audra was rendered speechless thinking about the reality of what Sara had just said. Just then J.P. emerged from the bathroom wearing his white shirt, black dress pants and black dress shoes. Audra's eyes opened wide when she saw J.P. She had never seen him wearing anything other than jeans and boots. "Wow, you look mighty handsome, cowboy!"

"Now, doesn't he just?" Sara grabbed Audra's hand. "Come on. I'll bring you to your dad. And you," she pointed to J.P., "we will see at the altar."

The innkeeper's wife had also made a small cluster of buds as a boutonnière for J.P. She pinned the buds to J.P.'s shirt when he came downstairs. "There," Nadia said, "now you're ready."

J.P. let out a small chuckle. "Thank you, Nadia." It was the closest thing he'd experience on his wedding day to having his mom there to look at him with pride.

J.P. went out to the back lawn where Cole, James, and Tanner met J.P. with handshakes and Casey greeted him with a peck on the cheek.

"So, are we still going to be able to have beers on the porch on a Friday evening every now and again?" Tanner asked.

"Nothing could keep me from the occasional evening drinking beers on the porch with my cousin." They grinned wide at each other.

With word that Audra and her father were ready, J.P. and Tanner took their places next to the Justice of the Peace. Sara stood nearby, her camera poised. William walked Audra to stand opposite J.P. After kissing her cheek, her father transferred her hand to J.P. to hold, then went to sit with Cole, James, and Casey. Tanner pulled the rings from his pocket when they were needed. Sara snapped photos throughout the short ceremony. Suddenly, they were married. J.P. kissed his wife, and with his forehead against hers, he looked into her eyes and said, "I am so happy." Audra started to cry, which became a mixture of laughing and crying. The moment was broken by her brothers rushing in to kiss and hug the bride. She saw that Casey and Sara were crying, which made Audra laugh. But she started crying again when her father stepped forward and wrapped his arms around her, pulling her into a big hug. "I love you, Dad." William pulled her head against his chest and kissed her hair. "I'm so happy for you, Audra."

"All I can hope is that we have a love as strong as you and Mom had," Audra said, and then everyone was crying.

They all gathered at the table on the inn's patio.

Holding his wine glass in front of him, J.P. addressed the table. "Thank you all for joining Audra and me today."

Glasses clinked as their guests held out their glasses, meeting in the middle over the table. As the group set their glasses back onto the table, Cole began to speak. "This is truly one of the best days of my life. To see my sister, so beautiful and so happy. We've always been close. You're a bright light in my life. I'm proud of you, Audra, for the wonderful woman you've become. I'm glad that you've found the man you truly love, and I know he handles your heart with care. So I don't worry about your being loved. I think I speak for my family, J.P., when I acknowledge with gratitude the unfaltering respect you've shown for our family in loving her." William and James nodded in agreement.

J.P. truly appreciated Cole's words and this was evident in his expression as he thanked Cole. J.P. added that his respect for the family came, in part, from his admiration of William, and though William may not know it, J.P. felt he had learned many valuable lessons from William.

"I've learned that when I make a decision and tell my staff, and eventually my children, what my expectations are of them, I then have to follow through with maintaining my expectations of them. Even if, as it was for me and Audra, it's challenging for them and even if, as I'm sure it was for…what do I call you now?"

William chuckled. "At work it's Mr. Becker still but with family it's William."

"Okay then…as I'm sure it was for William, even if it's hard to watch them work through to the goal." William nodded at J.P. "I also learned a lot about scotch," J.P. joked.

Tanner then reminisced about Audra as a child, one whom he believed to have grown to be a remarkable woman with the help of three dads—four, if you included Tanner. Audra said that she most definitely included Tanner when she thought about the people who had helped to shape her to be the person she was. Tanner smiled and continued. "Maddie couldn't be here to help raise Audra…" He stopped to collect himself. "But her spirit is unmistakably evident in her daughter." Tanner looked at William, then moved on to avoid the tears welling up in his eyes. "And my stud-muffin cousin is…no fool." Everyone laughed. "He knew that putting aside his desires and waiting for Audra was the right thing to do and that she was going to be well worth the effort. I can certainly vouch for the superhuman effort this man put into struggling to wait for her. I couldn't be happier for two people whose journey, though trying, has led them to be exactly where they want to be." Tanner raised his glass in their honor.

"Stud-muffin cousin, that's what you said, right Tanner?" James teased.

"Hey, it's his wedding…" Tanner defended his comment, laughing.

"Well, Tanner can joke about his cousin but there's no joke about J.P.'s integrity. As for his wife, I'll admit it, I'm going to miss that little snot around the house."

"Yes, he calls me 'little snot'," Audra admitted with an endearing smile for James.

"Well, I'm looking forward to many 'mini snots'…and 'mini stud-muffins'," James joked.

"I'm with James," William said. "I'm looking forward to grandchildren—I can't believe I'm old enough to say that!"

"Oh, when you said that you were with James, Dad, I thought you meant you were going to miss the little snot around the house!" Cole joked.

"Excuse me, it's Mrs. Ryan, if you please!" Audra spoke up. Again everyone laughed.

Nadia served the salad, and Clement poured his homemade lemonade. The family ate, laughed and reminisced through a simply elegant meal on the patio of the inn in the Smokey Mountains. Someone suggested coming back every year from now on, as a family. Nadia had made a special wedding cake for dessert. It was her and Clement's gift to the couple, as Audra had not specifically requested a wedding cake. Everyone agreed it was the most wonderfully moist strawberry cake. Nadia topped it with clouds of real whipped cream.

"Tanner?" Audra called across the table for his attention. "This reminds me of the strawberry pie you made me for my seventeenth birthday. I'll never forget that."

Tanner smiled at Audra. Casey leaned over in admiration and kissed Tanner on the cheek. "I see that I'm not the only woman you have spoiled!" Casey teased Tanner.

"Speaking of spoiled," Audra began, "would those stunning diamond earrings be a gift from Tanner?"

"In fact, they are." Casey looked lovingly into Tanner's eyes.

"Fiftieth birthday." Tanner teased.

Casey's mouth dropped. "Tanner! I am not fifty!"

"Gosh, all I got for my birthday was strawberry pie!" Audra shot back.

"I guess you'll have to wait until you turn fifty, Audra." Casey was learning how to retort to being teased by Tanner. He beamed at her with pride, wrapped an arm around her shoulders and pulled her in close.

"No, seriously, Tanner, those are absolutely stunning," Audra complimented. Everyone agreed.

William leaned over to James and whispered, "Why do I have the feeling I could lose some good staff to women?"

"Because you hire men that look like Adonis," James replied flatly.

"Do I?" William began thinking about the men who worked for him.

"I think any real cowboy is sexy as hell," James professed.

"Yeah?"

"Yeah, Dad."

"Elena?" William pursued the topic.

"I also can't resist a beautiful woman."

"I admire your honesty—with yourself and that you feel you can be open with me."

"I don't feel I have anything to be ashamed about, and I know you love me. Thank you for being accepting. Otherwise, I think I'd be tormented for the rest of my life trying to keep it a secret. While we're on the subject, do you think you'll be okay with the fact that I don't plan to have the wife, house with a white picket fence and standard 2.5 kids?"

William looked at James. "Be happy. That's all I want for my children."

James gave his father's shoulder an appreciative squeeze.

The family began to say their goodbyes. They praised Nadia and Clement on their wonderful meal and commented on the serene setting of the inn. Everyone agreed they had felt welcomed and would like to return someday. Hugs and well wishes were passed around amongst the family, leaving Audra and J.P. to enjoy their weekend away.

Almost as soon as Cole drove onto the highway after leaving the inn, Sara was asleep. His mind started to wander as he drove the many miles to Sara's family's home. On the top of his mind was wondering why the news that Audra and J.P. would be living in the small house bothered him so much. It was the obvious ideal situation for them. Nonetheless, Cole wanted him and Sara to live there and he let it bother him all week. Things like the two hour drive between Bridgeton Pass and Sara's family's farm was something he wasn't sure he'd ever get used to. He felt selfish that he wished he and Sara would live at Bridgeton Pass after they were married. Cole couldn't deny that those were his true feelings. Logically, living at Sara's family's farm made sense but that didn't mean he liked the thought of it. That it was okay to feel this way was something he was beginning to accept. It didn't mean he didn't love Sara, because he did. In fact, it was because he loved her that he agreed to live at her family's farm. Sara's mother was not at all well, and she was the sole reason they would be living there. Her mother was adamant she would not leave their farm to live at Bridgeton Pass. Cole could understand the woman didn't want to leave her homestead in her dying days. And there was no way he would ever ask her to leave her mother and live two hours away at Bridgeton Pass. If there was a good side to it all it was that there was the knowledge that they may not need to live there for too long a time. Cole didn't want to believe he could wish his future mother-in-law to pass away. It scared him to think he could be that kind of person. Instead, he tried to think about Sara and how hard it was for her to watch and care for her dying mother. Cole remembered helping to care for his mother, and then his grandparents before each passed. He remembered it wasn't easy, and he wasn't looking forward to helping to care for a woman he hardly knew, even if it was his fiancée's mother. Cole selfishly wanted it to be his turn in life to be alone with someone who cared for him. Even if it was for just the short while until they had children.

Just within the past month or so, Sara's mother began to require increasingly more assistance. Sara and her sister, Beth, managed to meet their mother's needs between the two of them thus far. Since Beth was married and had two young children, Sara was the primary live-in caregiver. So when Sara asked Beth to stay with their mother, such as when Sara stayed at the Beckers for Christmas, Beth was as accommodating as she could be. Cole and Sara had talked and decided that Sara would not continue to work after they got married. Financially, she wouldn't have to, which would be convenient as it allowed her to care for her mother full-time. Also from their discussions, Cole knew Sara didn't want to wait to have children. She hoped to start their family right away. Thinking about their life together as much as he was lately, Cole had come to realize he was going to marry Sara but would never live any amount of their married life just being a couple. Cole didn't want that. He wanted to have time to grow together before bringing children into their lives. He wanted to be selfish and love just Sara. Not Sara-the-mother or Sara-the-mother-in-law's-caretaker. He wanted her all to himself. Searching the internet and even a conversation with Audra's former nurse, Casey, Cole found that a private nurse might be the answer. Sometime before they get to Sara's family's farm today, he would talk to her about the idea.

A while later, he looked over at Sara sleeping in the passenger seat. She was beautiful. His life was with her. Then she began to stir. A small squeak came from her when she yawned while stretching. The sound stirred a warm feeling within him and made him smile.

"Hey, beautiful. How was your nap?"

"Great." She rolled the kinks from her neck. "That was such a wonderful wedding, wasn't it?"

"It was. I'm so happy for Audra and J.P."

"Mmmm. We're planning our wedding. Isn't that amazing, Cole? I can't wait to marry you! To be the bride." The smile on Sara's face reflected her thoughts off in the distance.

"I'm glad you're enjoying planning our wedding. It's going to be fabulous, I just know." He reached across the front seat and gave Sara's hand a squeeze. "Sara, I have something I want to talk to you about."

"Oh? What is it?"

"I've been thinking about you and your role in caring for your mother. I wish that you and your mother could spend her last days as mother and daughter. I would love for your time together to be quality time, reliving and making memories and not so much as time when you are caring for her. So I did a little research and what I found is that there are some options in regards to having a private nurse come into the house to help. I'd like to share the information that I do have, but I have to know you understand I am not suggesting this because I don't have faith in your abilities or dedication to care for your mother."

A flood of different feelings washed over Sara, almost drowning her. She tried to sort through them. There was an immediate panicked feeling that she wouldn't be capable of caring for her mother as her mother's condition continued to deteriorate. But Cole explained that was not how he felt. Then she tried to imagine presenting this idea to her mother and all the different ways her mother could interpret Sara's intentions with such an idea. "I guess I'll have to think about it, Cole." It was quiet during their car ride while Sara pondered the idea, then asked, "Would this person live in the house with us?"

"I've only gathered some cursory information about this sort of thing thus far. What I've found is there are different levels of support a service like this can provide, depending on the patient and their family's needs. Like I said, I didn't research the topic enough to feel I have all the information about it. Just some basic information is all I have."

"But, Cole, it's got to be quite expensive. Mom needs care 24/7." This concerned Sara greatly.

"Well, apparently there are services that she may qualify for through her health insurance." He didn't want to tell her just yet that he would be able to fund a private nurse without the help of insurance, if needed. He didn't want Sara to feel he was overstepping her family's decisions or that her family needed his money. He planned to offer that option only if they found that she didn't qualify for assistance.

"I think one of her doctors mentioned something about this a while ago. I wasn't quite at the point where I was accepting that my mother would need such services at the time, so I didn't really pay attention to the information he was trying to give me. I could ask him to go over it with me again."

"Sara, I want you to pursue this only if you feel comfortable with doing so. I'd hate for you to make any changes then feel like I pushed you into doing something that you didn't want to."

"No, I understand what you said, about spending my mom's last days as mother and daughter. Though you know I would and will care for her to the end. I'm finding that it would be helpful to have some outside assistance." Sara looked at Cole. "Thank you for thinking of us the way you do. This is one of the many reasons I love you so much." Tears started to well in her eyes.

While Cole took Sara home to her family's farm, James went to Greenville for a well-deserved long weekend away. As he sometimes did, James checked into one of the nicer hotels in the city, dressed to kill and went clubbing late into the night. Sometimes he made plans and met up with friends. Sometimes he just went to meet new friends. That weekend he had been caught on a local reporter's camera coming out of a known BDSM club. The photo itself was harmless appearing. The media apparently felt this to be newsworthy and played off the farm's losses in the fire and attempted murder of Jericho to sensationalize the information. Unfortunately, two potential buyers decided to take a stand against James' alleged lifestyle by taking their business elsewhere. The loss of a sale of one horse had cost the farm greatly, two had been real bad. Cole wondered how he would possibly restore the farm's good reputation. He had been talented in his marketing skills but all of the recent bad publicity tested his abilities, even if he had not had the pressure of his wedding coming up in two weeks.

Cole met with his father and James the Monday afternoon the newspapers highlighted Bridgeton Pass Farms' troubles.

"I called the police this morning. The guy who was in

the barn on Saturday night admitted to being hired by Eddie. But it seems that Eddie may have fled the area. The authorities have been unable to locate him."

They each looked to the other and nodded their reluctant acceptance of the news.

"You're going to have to make some statements, Dad. With the papers and the local television news stations. I'll get Melissa on setting those interviews up," Cole continued.

"You're right, Cole. I'll have to assure the community that there will be no more incidents at the farm, even if I can't guarantee it, and support James in his right to his personal life."

"Thanks, Dad," James said. "I'm sorry if my—"

William's voice was stern in cutting James off. "No, James. Don't apologize for people who judge others unfairly."

On the following Sunday afternoon, the week before Cole's wedding, the Beckers had gathered at the main house for dinner.

"Hey, how's the happy couple?" Today was the first time Sara had seen Audra and J.P. since they were married.

Audra ran into Sara's outspread arms. "Thank you so much for all you did at the small house!" Audra was referring to the "Just Married" decorations and the pre-made meal Sara had left in the refrigerator there to have when they returned from their mini honeymoon.

"Oh, you're welcome. I figured you weren't going to want to cook at least the first night you were home."

"It was wonderful of you. Thank you." Audra waggled her eyebrows as she said this.

"Yeah, Cole, Sara ain't too bad a cook judging by that meal. Lucky dog, you are!" J.P. winked at Audra as he praised Sara.

"Only one more week until your wedding." James looked from Cole to Sara, who were smiling. Sara giggled.

"I've had to taste-test all the different foods options. The caterers made us go to their office last Wednesday and make all kinds of choices."

James laughed. "I bet that was difficult, Cole. As your Best Man, I would have stepped up to that 'plate' for you."

"Oh my God, you are such a geek, James!" Audra exclaimed at her brother's lame humor.

"Because I am the King of Puns or because I'm a nice, helpful brother? Huh, which is it, snot?"

Audra rolled her eyes. "Well, I think we all are dying to know, Cole. Will there be a cheese log appetizer?"

"No! Absolutely not." Sara was adamant.

"Now, wait a minute…" Cole attempted to interject.

William sat back and listened to the mayhem surrounding him. Having finished his meal, he wiped the corner of his mouth with his napkin.

"Don't worry, bro'. I've got you covered." James gave Cole a small nod.

Sara pointed her knife at James as she spoke. "You are not bringing a cheese log to our wedding, James! I'm serious!"

William rose from the table, getting everyone's attention. "I'm going to the living room for an digesttif. Anyone care to join me?"

In the living room, they had all lounged on the couches and chairs.

"Sara and I ran into Tanner and Casey at the diner downtown earlier this week," Cole announced.

"Casey's a doll," Audra said.

"I really like them. They seem like a real nice couple," Sara added.

"Given his self-proclaimed permanent bachelor status, I was surprised to find out he had started dating someone,"

William said.

"I was surprised as well," James agreed.

"They seem pretty content being together. I'm happy for Tanner," Cole said.

James asked Sara about her family's farm. She had provided the technical details that she assumed James was interested in.

"And your family? Does everyone still live at the farm?"

Sara had explained that her father had passed away several years ago and that she had only an older sister, Beth, who was married with two young children. She told James that her sister lived at one end of the family property, about a mile from the farm's main house. There, she went on to explain, was where her mother lived alone until Sara had moved back to her family's farm from an apartment in Greenville a few years ago. She had done so because her mother was aging and ill. Sara had looked at Cole with admiration when she explained how lucky she was that Cole was so giving to agree to live at Sara's family's farm after their wedding. She had known it wasn't ideal, for either of them.

"My love did recently mention the idea of getting a private nurse to help care for my mother. I'm looking into that now."

"That sounds like an ideal plan," William interjected.

Audra had asked Sara about some details of her and Cole's wedding and soon they had been deep in discussion. The men had ventured to the game table. James suggested a game of friendly poker. William had retrieved the chips and J.P. had dealt the cards while Cole had filled drink orders. A few times during their game they had become so loud with laughter and accusations of cheating that the women had stopped talking only to roll their eyes and return to their conversation.

Eventually, James had informed the group that he would need to leave the game after the next hand to pick up a date with whom he had made plans for the evening. The relaxed feeling at the game table instantly became tense. Other than the brief conversation that William, Cole, and James had the Monday morning after the media fiasco, the family had not had any discussions. William had, later that Monday afternoon, made a vague blanket statement for the news media stating that the farm had been the victim of some malicious activity, though the activity was now under control. When questioned by the media about the effect of James having been photographed coming from the BDSM club on the farm's business, William simply stated it had been business as usual.

James opened his mouth to speak, ready to defend himself if needed. William spoke first. "It's unfortunate that someone thought to use media to incite fervor about an occurrence that has no story behind it. James knows this is a business that we run, one that supports this entire family. The integrity and reputation of the farm is an integral part of its success. Plus, he just completed a difficult program to obtain his master's degree. I'm sure he intends to use it."

His father's words were both supportive and a warning. Aware of the weight his father has put on the farm's reputation and how unrelenting he was in his sister's affairs, James spoke with what he hoped reflected great respect. "I understand, Dad. Please, I assure you," James paused to make eye contact with his brother and J.P., "I have been as discreet as Cole and Audra have been in their relationships. I am very aware that the reputation of this business goes deep and its face must be kept clean. I hope that you all will continue to trust me and my judgment. Also, it is my hope that you all feel comfortable with me and know that you can speak freely to me of any concerns or questions you may have."

"Of course, James," Cole spoke for himself.

J.P. assured James of the same.

"Dad, what about you?" James asked.

"James, I do trust you, implicitly. I would not have you by my side running this business with me if I did not. And to dismiss you would be a gravely difficult thing to do." William's face was stern. "I want you, I want all my children, to live their lives as they choose and be happy. I also expect that they are respectful adults and business partners." He looked to each of them. All agreed. There was no further discussion. James excused himself to leave for his date.

William asked Audra and Sara to join the men remaining at the table.

"I'll let James and you all speak for yourselves as you're comfortable doing so. James has been honest with me for some time about his preferences. I just wanted to say that James has spent some time sorting himself out. I'm very proud of how honest and accepting he has been of himself. You realize that James could have spent a long time, if not his whole life, lying or not accepting who he is. I've left my door open for him to talk to me about whatever he wanted. I could never shut my door on any of my children, no matter what. His lifestyle choices do not concern me. As with any of my children, your choices become concerning when or if the choices affect business. Now, Cole and J.P. have just assured James that they feel they can talk to James about any concerns or questions they may have. I need to ask you, Audra and Sara, if you feel that you could do the same."

Both Audra and Sara said they were comfortable with and accepted James no matter what his personal choices were. Cole then stood and announced the need for him and Sara to begin the drive back to her family's farm where he would stay the night before heading back to Bridgeton Pass to work in the morning. Yawning as if to prove her fatigue, Audra was tired, and so she and J.P. went back to the small house.

During the last week before the wedding Sara's two aunts, Lydia and Catherine, and her sister, Beth, had been at the Beckers' farm often to help Sara make last minute arrangements and preparations. Since Sara had arranged hospice services for her mother to supplement the help that Sara and Beth had been providing thus giving their mother twenty-four hour care, Sara and Beth were able to travel to Bridgeton Pass each day with the women. The seating chart had been made and favors were crafted. Audra helped as well and on the last day they had a small wedding shower for the bride.

William had kindly provided lunch each day for the ladies. He had figured it was the least he could do given that the original plan had been for the women to stay in the small house that week to avoid the long drive to and from the Columbia area where they all lived. But since Audra and J.P. were now married and living there, the women had no choice but to resort to the daily commute. William used the same catering service that Sara had arranged to use for the wedding to set up lunch outdoors on the lawn each day for the ladies. William stopped by each day to make sure that lunch was adequate as well as to be cordial to Sara's family, guests on his property.

Given Sara's mother's inability to host a rehearsal dinner, and the lack of large restaurants in the rural areas of each of their farms, William offered to host the rehearsal dinner at the Becker farm. Sara insisted that her family cover the catering for the event, only allowing the Beckers' to offer the use of the lawn outside the small house. Sara arranged for the rehearsal dinner to also be provided by the same catering company as the one being used for the wedding. It was convenient that the tent, tables and chairs could be set up for the rehearsal dinner and left there to be used for the wedding the next day.

Bubbling with excitement and a little nervous, Sara arrived at the rehearsal dinner with her Aunt Catherine a little early. Sara's aunt would be giving her away at the wedding the next day. Spotting Cole at the appetizer table, Sara hurried to him at first forgetting about her aunt. When she looked back, Sara saw her aunt was chatting happily with Mr. Becker. Sara smiled and turned back to Cole, who welcomed Sara into his arms and pulled her close for a kiss.

When dinner was ready to be served, the guests found their seats and began to sit at the tables. A silly grin was pasted across Sara's face all evening, she was just so happy. The usual cool aloofness of her aunt Catherine was more like an arctic front when her aunt took her seat next to Sara. Sara's grin immediately dissipated.

"What's wrong, Aunt Catherine?"

"Nothing dear, why do you ask?"

"Um...I...are you sure you're okay?"

"Yes, dear. Now stop your fretting." Her aunt picked up her napkin and placed it in her lap before turning back to Sara with a smile.

Sara nodded to her aunt, unconvinced. Though she had noted her aunt to be quiet and sullen the remainder of the evening, Sara chose not to pursue the matter. Her aunt would talk to her if she felt it necessary. Of that, when it came to her surly aunt, Sara had no doubt.

Following the rehearsal dinner, Sara drove herself and her Aunt Catherine home. But before she did, Cole held Sara and whispered a desire to not let her go.

"You'll see me tomorrow and then I'll be your wife."

"I know, but I still don't want to let you go tonight."

"Kiss me."

His warm lips fell softly to hers. He slid them smoothly to nibble on the corner of her mouth. He smelled like beer and tasted a little sweet, probably from the pie served at dessert.

"I'd better let you go before I take you right here." His hands slid down to her waist and he pushed her gently away from him. *Tomorrow,* he thought, *she will be all mine.* Cole held Sara's door open for her and helped her in, then did the same for her aunt. Once they had driven away, Cole joined his family in the living room of the main house. He had asked them to spend some private family time together after the rehearsal dinner. They spent an hour or so gathered around the game table remembering Maddie. They looked through photo albums and other mementos together. From the evening, Cole got what he needed to be able to face the wedding day without his mother.

The weather had been rather consistent that summer so there was no worry that the wedding day wouldn't be anything but perfect. Especially nice was the slight breeze that came across the lawn occasionally throughout the day, making the heat of the sun more bearable.

Inside the small house, J.P. ran his hands over the silky material of Audra's bridesmaid dress while she put on her earrings in front of the bathroom mirror. He slid his hand over her flat stomach and thought how he anticipated the day when he would instead feel the bump of a child. He gave a soft kiss on her neck, rested his chin on her shoulder and looked at her in the mirror. It was a favorite thing to do, watch his wife from behind her in the mirror as she got ready to go out. To J.P., it was one of the sexiest things to watch.

"You are so beautiful. I didn't know it was possible to love someone this much."

"Stop, you'll make me cry and then I'll have to re-do

my makeup!"

"Well, then if you'll have to be re-doing yourself, why don't we—"

"J.P., go and get ready. You'll be late for the wedding if you keep this up." He had his pants on with the suspenders hanging down over his hips but nothing more. *I'd suggest he take a cold shower if I didn't know that he already took one.* When he did finish dressing, he was so very handsome in his tuxedo, Audra thought. "Now I need a cold shower," Audra said under her breath as they walked out the door to the lawn.

"What's that, darlin'?" J.P. asked. He had a devilish smirk on his face. He slowed a step to let Audra catch up to him and slid his arm around her shoulders. He leaned in next to her and whispered in her ear as he slid his hand down over her buttock and gave a gentle squeeze. Audra shot him a glance, telling him to behave. He looked at her innocently as he bit his bottom lip, then kissed her forehead.

The ceremony was traditional and simple. It was in line with Sara's simple white wedding gown and flowers. Sara's aunt, Catherine, as the closest living and able related elder had given Sara away. She walked the bride to the waiting minister and Cole. A wedding video had been made to show Sara's mother at a later time.

Similar to the set up for Manuel's retirement party, tables and chairs were arranged under a large tent for the reception. A band played music and next to them a temporary dance floor had been placed over the grass. The bride and groom sat at a table set just for them. Sitting at a table nearby were J.P., Audra, William, James and his new girlfriend, Savine. Audra almost felt bad for Sara as no one could take their eyes off of Savine. She had such natural grace and beauty, it hadn't been a surprise when she said that she was a model. Audra and J.P. received many congratulations on their recent marriage from family and friends who stopped by the family's table. They began to make small talk about Sara and Cole's ceremony. Luckily, salads then began being served. J.P. could hardly keep his hands off Audra. He was conscious of this and worked hard to maintain a respectable level of discretion. At one point during the meal he even tried sitting on his hands. He felt like a horse just out of the gate when the meal was over, and the band started to play. Bolting upright from his seat, he stood and asked Audra, "Dance with me?"

"No way am I getting on the dance floor with you in front of everyone's eyes right now, you can't keep it together." She lowered her voice, "I'm going to use the bathroom in the main house..." She rose from her seat and walked away. J.P. waited a few minutes before he left the tented area and went to the main house.

James was talking to Cole when Audra and J.P. returned to the reception.

"James was just telling me a little about Savine." Cole brought Audra and J.P. up to date on their conversation.

"I was telling Cole that he can be sure Savine is someone special to me, otherwise I wouldn't have brought her to my brother's wedding. A sibling's wedding is too personal and special an event to take just any date to."

Audra's smile widened. "So, you really like her, huh, James?"

"Yes." The look in his eyes as he watched her moving across from them in the tent told it all.

"Does she live local? I mean, why would a model live out here?" Audra asked.

"She has a few apartments in different countries." Just then Savine slid in close to James' side. Each placed an arm around the other's waist. They briefly stared into each other's eyes, a whisper of a grin tweaked Savine's full lips, then James asked her to dance. James matched her model height, even with stilettos on. Their bodies fit nicely together, his muscular athletic build complementing her graceful frame.

"Woo-by gees, they are hot." Audra fanned herself.

Cole smiled and returned to his bride.

"Mrs. Ryan, I want that dance you wouldn't give me earlier." J.P. led Audra to the dance floor and with a half twirl pulled her in close, his lips just brushing her ear. "Can you wear this dress more often? I like the way it feels on you." Along the length of her back, his large hand glided over the silky material.

"What, like, when I vacuum?" Audra joked.

"Yeah, why not?" J.P. teased back at her.

She rolled her eyes at him. "It's nice to not have to pretend anymore, J.P. We can dance without having to hide in the shadows."

"It sure is, baby. It sure is." He buried his face in her hair and pulled her in even closer. The song ended, and they left the dance floor holding hands.

Sara was happy with the wedding in the end and that made Cole happy. What hadn't made Cole happy was the lack of a honeymoon but the immediate start of a daily two hour commute each way for work. As it happened, Cole was able to do some work from home, however, that meant being in Sara's family's home with his mother-in-law, and all of the people coming and going to care for her while he tried to work. He did his best to try to think on the bright side. By working from home he had the opportunity to have lunch with Sara on those days. It didn't last long before even that thought didn't help the situation as a whole.

August 2012

Missing Audra came as a surprise to Cole. Working in the farm's offices provided him the opportunities to interact with his father and James on a fairly regular basis. With Audra, opportunities like that were much less frequent. About a month after he had been married, Cole came up with an idea. While talking to J.P. at lunch in the office one Friday, J.P. had mentioned he was going to have beers on the porch at the Farm Hand House with Tanner that evening. Cole thought to invite himself to have dinner with Audra and J.P., then stay and spend some time with Audra while J.P. spent time with his cousin. Everyone liked the idea.

Audra made salad and a pizza for dinner. J.P. and Cole walked into the small house from the offices that evening just as the pizza was coming out of the oven. J.P. ran upstairs to wash up before dinner after hugging and kissing his wife. Cole used the first floor bathroom, then joined them at the table. J.P. was setting cups on the table. Audra thought Cole looked tired. She imagined the commute was at least part of the reason. Her brother sensed that she was staring at him. He gave her a weary smile.

J.P. cleared his plate and cup when he had finished and excused himself to go spend some time with his cousin. He gave Audra a kiss on his way out and told Cole he'd see him at the office on Monday. Cole helped Audra clear the rest of the dinner dishes, then they sat in the living room together. It was dark outside early in the evening at this time of year and that made Cole feel even more tired. Audra asked him about it. As she had figured, Cole was finding the adjustments to his work schedule and daily life difficult, including cutting into time he usually spent asleep. He also explained that he was feeling the stress of having twenty-four hour staff ever present in the house for his mother-in-law. Similarly, Sara hadn't slept well since having staff in the house and now someone else in her bed, which translated into another reason Cole was not sleeping very well.

"It's really not as bad as it all sounds when I talk about it. It's more a matter of getting used to some changes in our lives," Cole told Audra.

"But, are you staying awake during your commute, Cole?"

"Yeah, we have an automatic coffee maker. On days that I commute, I grab my coffee before I drive in the morning." They were quiet for a moment. "Audra, let's make a deal that neither of us will make the other care for us when we get old. I don't want my family to have the burden of caring for me, feeding me, giving me my meds, none of it. I've done it one too many times in my life. I couldn't make anyone in my family do that for me. And, honestly, as much as I love you, I couldn't watch you die in front me while knowing that I also had to change your diaper. You know?"

"I'll trust you, Cole. I mean, it doesn't sound like a fun way to live life," Audra replied. "Though, I did have to have you guys help to take care of me after the riding accident. That wasn't so bad, was it?"

"That was different, Audra. You were temporarily out of commission. Not needing full-time care, totally dependent on someone else to keep you alive," Cole explained.

"I can see what you're saying. Boy, this is a real trial for you and Sara, and right out the gate after your wedding." Audra's expression was pained thinking about her brother's troubles.

Cole explained how Sara had been living on her own, in her own apartment when they met. She moved back to her family's farm shortly after they had met. It wasn't long after meeting her that he knew that he loved Sara. They knew a relationship was going to be tough, but they decided they would go through the tough times together. It didn't take long for Cole to see how tough a time it would be. Cole told his sister that he struggled with himself constantly over trying to be the support for Sara and despising their life. He pointed out that they didn't get to go on a honeymoon because of her mother's needs.

"Cole, you love Sara, but you also love loving her. She's right there with you every day now, but you still can't love her the way you want to. You will have a lifetime of that love that you want, you just can't have it right now. Does that sound familiar?" Audra asked. She could see that Cole was making the connection that his current troubles were parallel to that which Audra had endured waiting to be old enough and for their father's blessing to have a serious relationship with J.P.

"Audra, sweetie, you're right. Wow. I knew those were difficult years for you. It was awful watching you go through that back then. And now…now I know what it was like for you, wanting what's there in front of you but you can't have it. This is real tough."

Audra got up from her chair and gave her brother a hug. "You'll be just fine," she whispered to him the same prophetic statement that Cole had told her many times over those years. "I'm going to make you some coffee for the ride home."

When Audra returned with a travel mug of coffee for Cole, he asked his sister how she was doing. He knew she had hoped she would be pregnant by now.

"I wish I were pregnant. It's what I've always wanted, to have children. I found my mate, my true love but now…it's not happening. It hurts. I'm frustrated and sad."

"I'm sorry, Audra. I wish I could change that for you and J.P. It has been your dream to have children for…forever."

"Cole, you've always wished that you could make everything right and perfect in my world. I love you for that." Audra had on a big smile for her brother that she adored. She wouldn't ask her brother. Especially when he's been married only one month, but she assumed that he and Sara were already trying to have a baby. She didn't have to ask.

"We're hopeful as well. Maybe you and Sara will become pregnant at about the same time." He tried to sound cheerful for his sister.

Her reply was laden with sadness. "Any time would be fine with me."

"I know, sweetie. I'd better get going. Thank you for dinner...and the coffee...and your support." Cole kissed his sister on her forehead and left. While he walked to his car, Cole passed J.P., who was walking back to the small house. They wished each other a good night.

November 2012

It had been almost four months after Cole had got married when while in his office at Bridgeton Pass Farms he got the call from Sara. Her mother had passed away. Hanging up the phone, Cole closed his eyes and sat back in his office chair. It was over. He felt as though the proverbial huge weight had been lifted off of him. And it disgusted him that he couldn't keep the edges of his mouth from curling even ever so slightly. He dry scrubbed his face with both hands and gathered himself for a moment before packing up his work and leaving the office to go be at Sara's side.

For the one and only time, he was happy to have the two hour drive to Sara's family's home ahead of him. The body would likely be gone by the time he got there. Cole thought of all the things he dreamed of doing with Sara countless times over the years but had not been able. Now, they would be able to live their life truly together. This was that "someday" he'd promised Sara she would have. That they would have. He couldn't wait to take her over the kitchen table, in the living room, anywhere and anytime he wanted. Shit, how much of an ass was he that he got a hard on because his mother-in-law died?

Everyone in the Becker family dealt with attending the funeral service in their own way. It was the first funeral the family had faced since Maddie's and then William's parents' deaths. Memories began to come back and unexpected feelings welled but overall, everyone did their best to make it through the day. Cole struggled to console his new wife while dealing with memories of his own losses. Memories of the deep sorrow he'd suffered when his mother died came flooding back. When his grandparents died he had been sad, truly sad for each of their passing, but there was also a sense of relief with his grandparents' deaths. He, at an age no kid should have had such responsibilities, spent so much time caring for them.

Sara was the most loving wife the day of her mother's funeral, letting Cole know that she was keeping in mind that he was most likely reliving some memories as well as trying to be supportive of her.

William suffered watching his son struggling with his own feelings and memories while trying to be supportive of Sara. He did his best to support Cole but all the while William was also dealing with his own feelings of being in a funeral home again and watching a graveside service.

Audra hadn't remembered much of her mother's or grandparents' passing and funerals. She found that she wasn't too fond of being in attendance at Sara's mother's funeral but afterward better understood her father's, brother's, and husband's grief. J.P. felt so far removed from this woman for whom they were having this service.

He understood the social graces of being there but nonetheless had his own demons to deal with and didn't like it.

James was probably the least stressed of everyone by the circumstances. He, by no means, wanted to be there, and that day conjured up sad memories, but James tended to have a more realistic, if not hard, grasp on life. He understood death for what it was, a ceasing to live. The family did what it was they always did, they supported each other and moved on.

* * *

And that was why Cole hadn't cared much for his mother-in-law. It was difficult for Cole to imagine the kind and caring person that Sara and her sister described their mother as having been before their mother became ill. The timing of his and Sara's meeting had been bad. Sara quickly became everything to Cole. It required significant patience for him to wait for the day when Sara could be his. And only his.

Part Two

November 2012

Immediately following the funeral, William began working with Cole on building a house for Cole, Sara and his future family on Bridgeton Pass property. And a few weeks after, Cole and Sara left for their delayed honeymoon, two weeks on a tropical island. Cole finally had Sara all to himself and loved every minute of it. They barely got out of bed. They stayed amongst tangled sheets and loved each other thoroughly. Sara was able to truly relax. Cole soon found that she was more responsive to his touches than she had been up until then. He reveled in the way he could make her body writhe beneath him, beg him for more and languished in her heated stares, hot licks, and whispered desires. They had been hot together in the beds they'd shared since they met but now, being together was beyond amazing. When they did leave their bed, Cole spent hours watching his beautiful wife as she lay peacefully in the afternoon sun. She wore a barely-there bikini that allowed Cole to admire her body as she walked along the beach and jumped through ocean waves. It also left so very much of her smooth, enticing skin bare for him to touch, lick, and kiss. He couldn't stop touching and admiring her. She was his.

He noticed her skin was beginning to tan by the fourth day when on the beach he helped her brush sand off of the backs of her thighs. Early in the evening, after having a margarita in the pool bar, the couple walked back to their hut on the beach holding hands.

"Shower and dress for dinner? Sound like a good plan?"

"Mmmm...sure does." Sara tossed her straw hat onto a nearby chair when they entered their hut.

Cole turned back from the windows where he had closed the drapes and saw Sara's pink sarong lying on the floor. He walked over to it. As he bent to pick it up he saw her bikini top lying on the floor a few feet away. He followed the trail of her clothing, leaving only the bikini bottoms to find. These lay on the floor outside the bathroom. Inside the shower water was running, and Sara was humming a tune. Cole pulled his T-shirt over his head and dropped it to the floor next to Sara's bikini bottoms. He stepped into the bathroom, pulled the string that held his swim trunks up, let them fall to the floor and stepped out of them. Through the frosted glass of the shower stall, he could see Sara turning her body under the spray of the shower head.

"Cole?"

"Yes."

Suddenly, Cole saw Sara's breasts pushed up against the frosted glass. Her nipples flattened and squished. Cole let out a loud laugh, and Sara started to giggle. He walked up to the glass wall and pretended to try and grab her breasts pressed up against the opposite side.

"Get in here!" she said through her giggles.

"You nut!" he joked and walked into the shower to join her. There in the shower her tan lines were undeniable. As water sprayed over their bodies, Cole traced her tan lines with a single finger, across her buttock, over her hip bone and down to the patch of pale curls between her thighs. Sara let out a moan thick with desire, threw her head back against his shoulder as he stood behind her and nipped at his earlobe. He coaxed her with teasing touches along her folds, soft kisses mixed with small bites at her shoulders and urging her to tell him what she needed. He slid one, then a second finger into her, circled her swollen nub with his thumb, and quickly she came for him. He smiled as he watched her break apart in his arms. Turning to face him, she pushed with both of her palms open flat on his chest until his back met the shower wall behind him. He could have sworn he heard her growl or maybe he just fantasized it. Either way it worked for him. She wrapped one and then her other leg around his waist. She was small, so he helped lift her and guided her to slide down onto him. Cole grinned to himself at the thought of his little jockey riding him so expertly. His grin tightened as did his balls just before he unloaded into her with a groan.

Sara was happy to be loved and spoiled by Cole. She knew he loved her so completely and never doubted he always would. And that's why it was so incredible when several weeks after they returned from their honeymoon her doctor confirmed they were going to be parents.

She began to think about all of the different feelings that her sister-in-law might have when Audra found out that Sara had become pregnant before her. Audra and J.P. had been married before her and Cole, they had been trying longer. Sara wanted to be the one to tell Audra rather than have her hear the news from her brother. She knew there was a part of becoming pregnant that Audra and Sara, as women, shared and that it would be hard for Audra to know that Sara would be having a baby before her. Sara went to the small house one weekday when she knew that she and Audra could be alone to talk. Sara was supportive of Audra and assured her that she understood when Audra cried.

"It's okay to be sad and even jealous," Sara said, offering Audra tissues. "I know you are happy for us, but you've been trying longer. I know how I would feel, and I want you to know it's okay to have whatever feelings that you're having."

"Oh, Sara, I am happy for you and Cole," she tried to smile through her tears, "but it does hurt a bit." She sniffed and wiped her nose. "Thank you for understanding, Sara. I love you." She hugged Audra and they cried together for a bit before Sara left.

Sara stopped in at the offices before leaving. Cole opened his arms and held her tight, knowing that it had been a hard talk for his wife to have with his sister. He admired Sara's graciousness. Cole and Sara then went to J.P.'s office.

"Got a minute?"

J.P. looked up from his work as he sat at his desk. He became concerned when he saw both Cole and Sara waiting at his doorway. "Sure, come on in. Have a seat."

Cole began, "We just wanted to tell you that Sara is pregnant."

"Congratulations!" J.P. came from behind his desk and hugged Sara, then shook Cole's hand.

Cole continued, "Sara just came from telling Audra the news. She wanted to tell Audra and give her the opportunity to talk to Sara about her feelings. We know that you and Audra want children very much and our news may be difficult to accept."

The feeling of respect and love of family was almost overwhelming for J.P. He swallowed the lump in his throat. "Thank you. That was very kind of you to be mindful of Audra's feelings. I'm sure she's as happy for you both as I am." J.P.'s smile was genuine and bright. He saw the sparkle of a tear forming in the corner of one of Sara's eyes.

"I'm going to walk Sara out to her car." Cole took a moment to stare at J.P. before turning to leave. He'd give J.P. some time to process the news, then check on him on his way back in from seeing Sara off.

"Are you okay?" Cole asked J.P. when he returned to

his brother-in-law's office moments later.

J.P.'s stare was focused on something across the room. "Yeah. It hurts a little but, of course, I'm happy for you guys."

"I'm sure." Cole didn't want to make assurances for things he knew nothing about. He didn't say anything more.

"We've both been tested by a fertility specialist and, medically, there's no reason we should have trouble conceiving. It just hasn't happened yet."

Cole felt like a weight had been lifted off his shoulders. "Thank you for sharing that information with me, J.P. That helps a lot. I had worried that infertility may be a problem for you both."

J.P. nodded his understanding before returning to his work. Having been dismissed, Cole went to his office.

December 2012

Sara and her sister, Beth, spent their afternoons over the next several weeks discussing pregnancy and marveling over Beth's newest baby while sorting through items in the family house.

"She's so beautiful, Beth." Sara held her new niece cuddled against her shoulder. She marveled at the baby's small features.

"I bet you can't wait for your baby."

"We are so excited. I don't think it's really hit me yet that I'm going to be a mother."

"It does take some time for it to become 'real,' but you will have no doubt as you grow bigger." Beth giggled thinking of her sister getting bigger with child. "Cole seems like he'll make a good father. His family is real close."

Sara handed her niece back to her sister and returned to removing items from one of their mother's dresser drawers. "He will make an awesome father. He really wants kids."

"I'm glad that you found him, Sara. He's a really great guy."

"Me too. He is pretty awesome."

"And hot! Whew, girl. Just think how gorgeous your kids will be."

Sara couldn't help but laugh.

Once the sisters had gone through the items in the house and kept those that each wanted, Cole arranged to have the unwanted items taken to charity. Beth and her growing family would be moving into the family house after the holidays. Sara was happy that she had had this time with her sister over the past several weeks, knowing that she would eventually be moving two hours away to the house being built at Bridgeton Pass. There were so many necessary decisions to be made when having a house built. The project had kept Cole and Sara busy. But with holidays coming up much of the work on the house had slowed. Sara and Cole would have to move into Cole's old room in the main house. Sara was glad for it as she was battling morning sickness. She was finding it hard to travel to Bridgeton Pass to meet with builders and contractors when she was feeling so sick. And though Cole tried to do as much as he could, some things required that both of them be present to make a decision.

It was Audra who came up with the idea to ask Casey if she would consider renting her house in downtown Carnegie temporarily to Cole and Sarah. Casey and Tanner were engaged and Casey would be moving into Tanner's apartment in the farm hands' house at Bridgeton Pass after their wedding. They had planned their wedding ceremony to be at the courthouse in town two days before Christmas.

Audra explained that living there would shorten Cole's commute. They would also be local, which would make it easier for them to meet with the builders and contractors working on their house. And everyone would feel better knowing Sara was close by as she advanced in her pregnancy. Casey thought it sounded like a good plan. She liked knowing that someone would be living in the house while she decided whether or not to sell it.

There had not been much moving to do to get Sara and Cole settled into Casey's house temporarily. The small bungalow was rented fully furnished. It had two bedrooms and one bathroom. Sara loved the living room the best. It was full of windows that flooded the room with sunlight and looked out onto the back yard. The house sat on a small patch of land, the back side of which bordered a narrow tract of wooded land with the town playground on the other side of it. Occasionally, they could hear the shouts and laughter of kids playing through the woods.

January 2013

The cool January morning air in the small bungalow's bedroom caused Sara to shiver when she got out of bed. She pulled her yellow chenille robe snug around her growing belly and stepped into her slippers. As she passed the bathroom on her way to the kitchen, Sara had caught sight of her unruly hair. It was in line with the tumultuous night's sleep that she had.

The coffee maker tormented her further. Its lid had recently begun to get stuck closed. She reached into a kitchen drawer and pulled out a meat mallet. After a couple of solid whacks the lid relented. Mentally, Sara added buying a new coffee maker to her list of things to do today. Only Cole was drinking coffee these days, but she usually made it. She wasn't going to fool with the old coffee maker anymore.

Thinking of her list of things to do, Sara decided to get a load of laundry started before beginning to make breakfast. While Sara sorted dirty clothing, she thought of how poor Audra, finally pregnant, was now fighting morning sickness while Sara was, on the other hand, continuously ravenous. She measured out laundry detergent and filled the machine with colored clothes, mostly jeans and T-shirts. Back in the kitchen Sara slid a couple slices of bread into the toaster, slapped a couple of slices of bacon into the cast iron skillet, set a frying pan on a stove burner to pre-heat, and poured two glasses of orange juice. Cole entered the kitchen as Sara was placing plates and silverware on the table. He greeted his wife with words of adoration and a sumptuous kiss. Sara warmed to her core at his touch. She leaned her backside against the kitchen counter, grabbed one of the glasses of juice that she had poured and watched Cole over the rim of her juice glass as she drank from it. He stood in front of the coffee maker wearing light blue cotton pajama bottoms with no shirt and bare feet, preparing his cup of coffee. Sara admired his muscular back and arms. He had just a sprinkling of freckles over his upper back. Cole took his coffee cup with him to the table.

"Are you checking me out, Sara?" he asked, wearing a slight grin.

Sara crossed the room and took two eggs from the refrigerator. "Shit, yeah! You can't swing eye-candy in front of a girl and not expect her to feast on it." She cracked the eggs onto the heated frying pan and flipped the bacon.

Cole leaned back in his chair at the kitchen table and stretched his arms across the backs of the chairs on either side of him. "Feast away, my dear."

Sara leaned over in front of him and slid an egg and some bacon onto his plate. She returned a moment later with buttered toast. Cole grabbed her around her waist. She leaned forward, and he kissed her. He held her there for a moment.

"Cole Becker, are you looking down my shirt?"

"Umm, yes," he said, never taking his eyes off of her chest. He reached into her robe, slid his hand under her shirt, and began to knead one of her breasts.

Sara rolled her eyes. "Eat your egg, then go take a cold shower. You've got twenty minutes to get to work." Cole's hand retreated, and he resumed eating.

"Fine. You just wait until I get home this evening," Cole countered.

"No, now I can't wait until you get home this evening!" Sara shook her head and laughed at Cole's antics.

Cole was ready for work and out the door within the twenty minutes available to him. Sara put the clean load of laundry into the dryer and set the washing machine to clean a load of bed sheets. She hummed a tune as she went back into the kitchen and cleaned the breakfast dishes. The bright sunshine poured in through the many windows of the little house and the air inside began to warm some. Sara made a cup of decaffeinated tea and sat in front of the expansive windows in the living room. She enjoyed the sun warming her face and sipped her tea before getting up to shower and moving on with her day.

Fresh from the shower and dressed, Sara grabbed her car keys and purse but decided to hang the load of clean sheets before she left the house to run her errands. She put her keys and purse back on the counter. In the laundry room, she loaded the wet sheets into the laundry basket and took the basket outside to the clothesline. Sara was looking forward to having fresh, clean sheets dried outdoors on her bed tonight. She felt it was one of those special little things in life that she liked to do for herself, like taking a bubble bath. She lifted a corner of a sheet from the laundry basket and reached up with a clothespin to pin it to the clothesline. Sara froze in place. Her heart beat wildly in her chest and her muscles tensed. A rough looking man stood three to four paces from her, watching her.

"I found you," was all he said.

Sara could feel her arms tremble, still frozen in the air ready to hang the sheet. Would he touch her? Who had he thought that he had found? She didn't know this man. Sara moved her eyes, searching for the basket of clothespins without moving her head. She contemplated how she might use the clothespins as a weapon. Sara tried to stay as still as possible, not knowing what this man would do to her. She heard the grass behind her rustle and turned to see him walking away from her. He stood along the back edge of the lawn just before the property turned into the wooded area. He held Sara's gaze with his piercing gray eyes. His face was expressionless. He stood motionless. His hollow form was dressed in dirty clothing that was torn in places. Without a word he slid into the wooded area behind the property.

Sara bolted into the house and locked the doors. She grabbed the cordless phone from its mount on the wall and hid in the bathroom, away from all of the windows of the house. Her heart was beating so fast it was hard for her to breathe. She stayed very still and listened carefully but heard nothing. It seemed that no one was trying to get into the house. She listened a little bit longer, her finger on the "9" of the dial pad on the phone ready to dial 911 if necessary. It was a good long while before Sara got the courage to move from her hiding spot. She moved slowly, trying to make as little noise as possible, keeping vigilant as she neared the closest window. She scoured the back yard with her eyes but saw no one. She did this as she went around the house. Satisfied, though scarcely, that no one was lurking outside, she grabbed her keys and purse and ran to her car. Once inside the car, she locked the doors and started the engine as fast as she could. She didn't care that the front door of the house was unlocked. She slammed the car into reverse and backed out onto the road, then drove away as fast as she could.

Sara was shaking so hard she was finding it hard to drive safely. She wanted to pull over and let herself calm down, but she couldn't, not until she got to the police station. In her car, parked in front of small town's police station, Sara turned off the ignition, leaned her head on the steering wheel and broke down. She reached into the glove box after a moment and grabbed some tissues she had stuffed in there. When she felt that she had pulled herself together enough to go into the police station, Sara wiped her eyes and blew her nose, then went in.

The officer took her information and the description that she gave of the man but given that he didn't do anything other than trespass and that he did leave the property, the officer told Sara there was not much more the police could do. Sara was hoping the description she gave of the man sounded familiar to the officer and that he might know who the man was, but apparently he did not. She thanked the officer and returned to her car. Sara sat in the driver's seat, trying to sort through her feelings. She knew she was new to living in the town but it was such a small town, why didn't her description of the man sound familiar to the officer? Had Casey ever seen this man before? If so, why didn't she tell Sara about him? She wondered if this was a onetime thing, a man just cutting through the property. Then she began to wonder if Eddie Fisher had anything to do with today's incident. Maybe she was over-reacting. Sara didn't care if she was or not, it scared her.

It was close to four o'clock in the afternoon when Sara finished running her errands. Her small car was filled with bags of cleaning supplies and non-perishable groceries. Cole would be at the office at Bridgeton Pass for probably another hour. She couldn't bring herself to go back to the house alone, especially since she had never locked the front door when she left the house earlier that day. She drove to Bridgeton Pass, hoping Audra would be home to visit with until Cole was ready to leave the office. Sara parked next to Cole's car and checked in with him in his office.

His door was open. Cole sat at his desk, engrossed in what he was working on. Sara knocked lightly on the door as she entered. Naturally, Cole was surprised to see her. He got up from his desk, came around and gave Sara a soft kiss but quickly knew something was wrong. Sara looked toward the open door of his office. Cole let her go from his embrace, then went over and closed the door. He led Sara to a chair and sat in the other one next to her, holding her hand. With worried eyes he looked at Sara and waited for her to tell him what was wrong. Sara related the details of her morning to Cole, then asked all the questions she had asked herself earlier. Cole thought that the officer may be new to the force, and even to the town. The name of the officer whom Sara had spoken to didn't sound familiar to Cole. To Sara's dismay, her description of the man she saw on the property didn't sound familiar to Cole either. Cole instructed Sara to go outside and check whether Casey's car was parked in her usual spot by the Farm Hands' House. When Sara returned moments later reporting that it appeared that Casey was home, Cole wrapped up his work at his desk, and they went to her apartment.

Casey welcomed Cole and Sara, inviting them to sit at the kitchen table while she prepared some tea for them. Curious, she asked the two why they had stopped in. Once Cole and Sara had told Casey the story, Casey confirmed that the officer whom Sara had spoken with today was new to town and its police force. Casey reminded Cole and informed Sara that her uncle was an officer in town. Sara instantly felt somewhat better to learn this.

"The man Sara described doesn't sound familiar to me but, Casey, do you think it's anyone you've seen in town?" Cole asked.

"It sounds like, by your description Sara, that it may be a fairly recent transient in town. I think his name is Vinnie. I've never seen him in my yard but have seen him on the streets around town, probably for the past three or four months. From talking about him with other locals downtown, he seems rather harmless," Casey spoke to both of them.

"You mean he's homeless? He just wanders the streets? Where does he sleep?" Sara sounded horrified.

"Yes, it appears that he is homeless. I don't know where he sleeps. He probably moves around, sleeping somewhere different every night or every few nights." Casey paused. She could tell that Sara wasn't comfortable with this situation. Sara looked up at Cole, who then put his arm around his wife's shoulders and gave her a quick hug in attempt to assure her things would be fine. "I'm going to call my uncle, ask him to have extra watch out downtown, and especially around the house, for this guy. There's a playground beyond the wooded area behind the house. He may have been just cutting across the property to get to the playground through the woods. But still, I don't think the community would like the thought of him hanging around the children in the playground either."

Though not relieved, Sara felt better to know that

someone at least recognized who the man was and that Casey would ask her uncle to have the police keep extra watch out around the house. Cole met Sara at the house and entered before her. Assuring her that the house was empty and safe, she began to unload her car of all her purchases. Cole checked that the property was also clear and finished hanging the sheets on the clothesline.

An officer called them later in the evening to check whether there had been any more unusual activity at the house. When Cole assured him that there had not been, the officer informed Cole that extra officers would be patrolling the downtown area, including around the house. He thanked the officer, and once off the phone, Cole hugged Sara close and reminded her they would only be there temporarily until their house was finished being built.

February 2013

The builder wanted to have some time to meet with Cole today. That was the message he got on his cell phone when he checked his voicemail after finally leaving his father's office. He had been meeting with his father for the past hour and a half. Cole checked his schedule and found that he had about twenty minutes open in his day but it would be in about one hour from now. He returned the builder's call, and they arranged to meet out at the building site. Now, he had to prepare the data his father had just spoken with him about. It was information that was badly needed, and compiled in a specific format. The office assistant, Melissa, knocked on his door. He was relieved to see that she just wanted to put some paperwork in Cole's in-box. That meant it wasn't something that needed to be done right away.

Meanwhile, back at the bungalow in town the smell of sugar cookies baking filled the kitchen. Sara put the last cookie sheet of neatly shaped mounds of dough into the oven and wiped her shirt sleeve across her brow. She wondered if she had just spread flour across her forehead. *That is a sign of a good baker, isn't it?* She smiled at the silly thought. Sara looked around the kitchen and imagined a little girl or boy, covered in flour, "helping" her bake cookies. She or he would have to stand on a chair pushed up close to the countertop to be able to reach the work surface. Her heart did a little flutter, and she began to clean up her baking mess. She carried the milk and butter to the refrigerator, then grabbed the sponge that was kept by the kitchen sink. With her hand still on the sponge, Sara lifted only her eyes, very slowly. Outside the window above the sink was the stranger staring back at her. The man who had trespassed that one time and that she had thought was gone. Looking into his eyes made her feel sick. The sponge fell from her hand. Her whole body began to shake violently. The sides of his mouth curled up ever so slowly, eventually revealing dark brown rot throughout the remaining yellow teeth his mouth held.

"That's my baby," he said.

"No!" Sara yelled and ran to the bathroom.

As she got sick into the toilet, Sara hoped he wasn't coming into the house. She willed herself to stop vomiting so that she could listen for any sounds of him intruding. When she did stop retching, Sara grabbed the doorframe of the bathroom with both hands to steady her and listened. She only heard the sound of the kitchen timer clicking away the minutes until her cookies were done baking. She peered out of the bathroom into the hall and saw nothing. It was still quiet in the house, so she slowly made her way to the kitchen but saw no one. No one was outside the window over the sink, looking in. No one was in the kitchen. Quickly, she made a sweep of the small house, checking every room and out every window. Again, she saw no one. Relief mixed with fear overtook her. Sara leaned against the wall in the living room and slid down to sitting on the floor. Tears flowed and she trembled. The kitchen timer went off. She needed to rinse her mouth.

Cole was getting frustrated. He knew that building a house always meant unexpected set-backs in the schedule and other headaches. But moving them from the rented house in town was foremost on Cole's agenda. Sara spent most days with Audra at the small house since the day Sara had seen the stranger watching her through the kitchen window. Cole and Sara were grateful to Audra, but it was inconvenient and they felt that they were being a burden, even though Audra assured them that the situation was not a burden to her. Cole was struggling with being told by the contractor that things were being held up again for yet another reason. Between the contractors and the local police, Cole was ready to pull his hair out. He had taken Sara to the police station after the last incident with the vagrant to file a report. They didn't think she would be able to get a restraining order against him as this had only been the second occurrence and he hadn't done anything malicious. Cole just needed for his house to be built.

One week later...

The office assistant, Melissa, had made it a habit to bring in one of her home baked coffee cakes or muffins to the office on Friday mornings. She had done this for the year and a half that she had worked in the Bridgeton Pass office. Melissa was in her early thirties. She lived alone and liked to spoil the Becker men with baked goods once a week, since they let her. As she poured water into the coffee maker, James came into the office kitchen and chose a piece of the lemon pound cake Melissa had baked. He made yummy noises as he ate, another reason Melissa liked to bake for the Becker men. They were very appreciative.

"The coffee will be ready in a minute, James. Don't you want coffee with your cake?" Melissa was always amazed how James was the first one to show up to sample her Friday morning fare, practically before she even got the plastic wrap off the plate.

"Sure, Melissa, I'll have some with my next piece." James was licking his fingers. Melissa handed him a napkin and shook her head.

"Did you already down a piece of that cake?" Cole asked as he entered the room. His brother didn't answer. James just sat at the table with a sassy grin, looking satisfied.

William joined them in the office kitchen when there was coffee available. Cole fielded the inevitable questions of when his house would be done that he had come to dread. He told them about Sara's recent ordeal with the stranger watching her. Melissa piped up when she heard this. She said that her friend, who lived in town, was unemployed and apparently knew everyone in town. She explained that this friend spent his days drifting from one business to the next talking to people, hoping for a lead on a job. Occasionally, he would run into Vinnie on the street, the stranger Sara had seen, and the two men would talk. Melissa recounted that her friend told her, two weeks ago, that Vinnie said he was leaving town.

"Wait," William interjected. "This Vinnie guy told your friend, two weeks ago, that he was leaving town?"

"That's what my friend said. He knows I live alone in town and am worried about Vinnie, given all that I had heard about him bothering Sara. Apparently, Vinnie told my friend that he was going to head further south and find somewhere else to live." Melissa pulled her coffee cup to her mouth and took a big gulp.

"Has your friend seen Vinnie since Vinnie told him this?" Cole asked.

"I don't think so." Melissa literally scratched her head while thinking. "I've seen my friend a few times since he told me this, and he hasn't mentioned Vinnie."

"Well, maybe he is gone," William said hopefully.

"I hope so, the police aren't too hopeful that Sara would be able to get a restraining order against him at this point," Cole said. He couldn't help but feel that there was still trouble looming.

"That stinks." James sighed. "Not to change the subject, but has there been any recent news on the whereabouts of Eddie Fisher?"

"Nothing. Rat bastard that he is," William griped. "I still have a private investigator looking for him but nothing yet."

After a collective introspective moment, J.P. asked James, "Hey, now that polo season is over, would you be interested in helping me some time to put together the baby crib we bought?"

"I'd love to. I'm fairly handy like that," James touted.

"That's why I asked you, James." J.P. didn't look up from his piece of cake.

"So, Cole, then you'll be taking the crib that's been in storage?" William asked. He had mentioned to Sara and Audra that he had stored a number of Cole, James, and Audra's baby things and suggested they take what they wanted.

"Yeah, thanks again, Dad, for allowing us to use the things in storage. J.P. and I perused the furnishings that were there in terms of safety since they've been unused for quite a while. Everything is still in good shape. It's amazing. He took the dresser and rocking chair, and I took the changing table and crib."

J.P. added, "I figured Audra would really like being able to use the rocking chair her mom rocked all her babies in."

James nodded his approval, and William expressed his appreciation of J.P.'s thoughtfulness. William agreed that he suspected Audra would like to have the rocking chair. "There were some clothes in there as well, did the girls find them?"

"Yes, I took the boxes of clothes to the small house so Audra and Sara could go through them. They each took a bunch of 'neutral' items like white T-shirts but are leaving the obvious girly and boy themed items to go through after the babies come."

"Well, good, I'm glad I kept those things then. It sounds like they'll be put to good use." William was decidedly happy with his foresight.

"I think having the crib is really cool. To think we all slept in it at one time," Cole said.

"I know I peed in it several times," James added.

Melissa rolled her eyes, took her coffee mug, and left the kitchen laughing.

Cole threw his waded paper napkin at James. "Nice," was all Cole said.

March 2013

"So, he really said 'that's my baby'?" Audra couldn't believe what Sara told her sister-in-law about the awful encounter.

Sara folded her clean laundry at the kitchen table in the small house. She was finding that it was better to talk about the encounter. Each time that she told the story it got easier for her let go of some of the feelings associated with it. "He must think I look like his wife or lover or someone, who knows? It's just all so creepy."

"It sure is. I'm so sorry, Sara. I'm happy you're here at the farm, though, we'd all worry too much if you weren't." Audra briefly touched Sara's shoulder in effort to provide some measure of comfort. She knew that Sara would rather be in her own house, safe, than hanging around her sister-in-law's house feeling like a burden. So, she changed the subject. "Looks like we're in for a big win coming up in April, huh? Isn't that great?"

"J.P. has really worked hard to get this horse up to its full potential. He was smart to vie for Miles Carney to jockey." Sara put the folded clothes into her laundry basket to bring home with her and Cole later that evening.

"Yes, that was a good move." Audra closed the refrigerator door. She could no longer rely on signs of hunger to remind her to start preparing dinner. Audra felt like she was hungry all the time these days. A quick look out the window confirmed dusk had not yet set in, but the clock on the wall told her it would begin within the next two hours. "I'm going into town in a few minutes. I want to get some items at the Farmer's Market. Any interest in coming along?"

"Sure. Sounds like fun."

Audra went directly to the table of asparagus when they arrived at the market. The local Farmer's Market was housed in an old building that sat by itself on a large plot in downtown Carnegie. As long as the weather was good, it was held mostly outside. Sara was amazed at the fresh vegetables piled on the tables set in long rows outdoors. Audra pulled Sara along by Sara's coat sleeve as she made her way through the maze of tables. She stopped occasionally to bag her selections, then headed to the cash register. The cashier weighed out Audra's items, gave her the total and took Audra's money. With her change and bag of produce in hand, Audra turned and began toward the parking lot. "Sara?" She looked around. There were a few people in the aisles at today's market so it didn't take her long to scan the entire area. "Sara?" she called a little louder this time. Still she got no reply. Audra went down a few rows, then began to scan the parking lot. Her heart began to beat faster. It all felt odd. How could she lose Sara so quickly and in such an open area?

"Are you okay, Audra?" Mr. Gendron, a kind older gentleman and longtime resident of Carnegie, asked. "You look like you've seen a ghost."

"Sara. Did you see a short blonde woman? I can't find her." Audra was truly panicking.

"The woman who was shopping with you?"

"Yes!"

"Only that I saw her with you. Don't see her around now."

"Thank you," Audra said brusquely and hurried to look around the building and surrounding area. She saw no sign of Sara and heard no reply to her repeated calls of Sara's name. She pulled out her mobile phone from her purse and with shaking hands dialed the police. At some point she had apparently started crying. A tear fell onto the screen of her phone as she dialed. Audra wiped her eyes with the back of her coat sleeve as she gave the police the information they needed. A moment later a police car pulled up to the market parking lot. Audra went to meet the policeman.

"She was there one minute and then…" she held her empty hands up in wonder "…then she was gone. You know that she's had trouble with some guy stalking her, right?" Audra couldn't believe what was happening and that it was her fault. What was she thinking taking Sara into town? The whole reason Sara was spending her days at the farm was to keep her safe. It wasn't safe for her to be in town. And she had brought Sara here. Now Sara was gone. Audra didn't want to think about where Sara could be or what was happening. Maybe Sara would just come walking from around the corner any minute, smiling and wondering what all the fuss was about. But Audra had a feeling of dread deep in her belly that that wouldn't happen.

"We've got a man patrolling the streets in his car. I'll give him the information and description that you provided. If we see her, we'll let you know," the officer said.

"That's it! *If* you see her! We have to scour the area before he takes her too far away! We can't just sit around and keep an eye out for her. She's pregnant, for God's sake!" Audra couldn't control her anger over the officer's nonchalant handling of the crisis.

"Ma'am, she could have just walked over to the grocery store for a pack of gum for all we know." The office offered as an explanation for his lack of alarm over the situation.

"Don't you dare think I'm just some overwrought pregnant woman making a big deal out of nothing! This is serious!" She could see that she was getting nowhere talking—or yelling—at this officer, and all the while this guy could be doing who knows what with Sara. She dialed Cole at his office at the farm. She really didn't want to tell him, but she was scared. She hoped she was worrying for nothing but didn't think that was the case. Sara wouldn't just walk off without saying something to Audra. And if she had told Audra she was going to be leaving her side, Audra wouldn't have allowed it.

Within forty-five minutes, Cole had rounded up every available employee at the farm. The group of vehicles with the men inside descended on the Farmer's Market parking lot. Since it had been only hours since Sara was apparently last seen, she wasn't considered a missing person, the officer explained, and thus a formal police led search would not be initiated at this point. With the help of the police officer, however, a plan was quickly devised where each vehicle would cover a different section of town and beyond.

"I heard this transient, Vinnie, had left the area, probably a few weeks ago," the officer said.

"I don't care who has her, I want her back!" Cole's stare was blank and his voice cold.

The officer and all of the men got into their vehicles and left to begin searching. Audra got into Cole's car and buckled her seatbelt.

"I'm so sorry, Cole!"

"Not now, Audra," he barked. "I know you didn't do anything or mean her any harm. I just have to focus on finding her right now."

Audra slumped in the passenger seat and looked out her window, searching for Sara.

* * *

The room was dark. It was not a room actually but the inside of the concession stand at the town's Little League baseball field, which also meant it had no heat. A shiver ran through her, causing her wrists to chafe against coarse, dry rope. Sara's hands were tied behind her back to a support under the stand's counter. She sat on the floor with her legs crossed. Being under the counter she was not able to stand up. Even if there were no counter over her head, Sara wasn't certain, being almost six months pregnant, that she could stand up from where she sat with her hands tied behind her back.

"Why are we here?" she asked her abductor.

"Shhh!" He shoved a wad of paper napkins into her

mouth. Dirt and grime were caked under his fingernails and within the creases of the cracked skin of his fingers. He sat next to her on the floor under the counter. The only windows were above the counter over their heads. No one would see them under the counter if just looking in through the windows. They'd have to open the door at the far end of the rectangular structure to see them. But Vinnie, she assumed that was his name, had locked and then barricaded the door with boxes of condiments and supplies.

He sat close enough to Sara that his thigh was leaning against hers. He looked to be about in his late thirties, though it was tough to tell given how dirty and worn his clothing and skin looked. The stench of his rotting teeth as he leaned toward Sara's face to whisper made her gag. She worked to expel the paper napkins from her mouth, only to have pieces stick to her tongue. She was able to loosen the wad from the back of her mouth somewhat to push it forward, but she decided to keep the napkin wad in her mouth. That way, she decided, she could spit it out at the last minute, and yell if an opportunity came along, without him suspecting anything.

"I got us a place to live. We'll go there and wait for our baby, Rachel. I'll keep you safe." Sara cringed as he ran his hand over her belly, stopping low over her mound to caress her there. Her body stiffened, repulsed by his touch. His steel gray eyes that before now had been piercing softened as he gazed at her. She recognized a spark of tenderness before his lips curled at the corners and his eyes reverted to the cold piercing stare.

Who was Rachel? He obviously thought that she was this Rachel person. This guy was delusional. Where was he planning on taking her? And more importantly, how was he planning on getting there? Sara tried to soften the look of her own expression and make this guy think that she was not going to fight him. Maybe she could get him to trust her enough that he'll let his guard down.

Suddenly, Sara could hear people talking, but they were too far away for her to make out what they were saying. It only lasted a moment and then it was quiet again. Obviously, she wasn't maintaining as good a poker face as she should. Her abductor slapped her across her face.

"Keep quiet, bitch. I'm warning you."

The sting lasted for a bit, but she had managed to remember to bite down on the wad of napkins and keep them in her mouth. She had to keep him thinking that she was effectively gagged. God knows what he would otherwise produce to gag her with.

"Don't even think of trying to get away from me, Rachel!" His face was suddenly close in front of hers, making her flinch. His anger flared but quickly abated. Vinnie sat back on his heels in front of her and said, almost tenderly, "Those people are not going to keep you safe like I will. You'll stay here with me."

The voices of people talking nearby could no longer be heard. She hoped that had not been her one and only chance and that it had slipped by. Would they come back? God, she hoped so.

Carnegie's downtown was only five blocks wide and six blocks long. It didn't take long for Henry and Tommy, two of the farm hands who volunteered to help, to search the alleyways, behind and in dumpsters and every other corner they could find along the streets they were assigned to scour.

"Nothing," Tommy said. "This isn't good. Either they're hiding real well down here in town or they've made it farther out." If they've made their way farther out of town, the men knew it would be much harder to find them.

184

"Let's call Cole and see what he knows. Maybe we can help somewhere else." Henry suggested.

Cole's hands were gripping the steering wheel of his car tightly. He was growing more anxious as time went on without finding Sara. It was also early evening now and dusk was upon them. He did not want to think about having to still try to find her after losing the light of day. Cole's mobile phone rang. He quickly picked it up from the car's center console.

"Hello. Okay." He ended the call. Audra was looking at him expectantly.

"It was Henry. They've found nothing downtown. He and Tommy are going to start driving outside the perimeter of downtown but close enough to check in downtown every now and again in case they missed them or they go back downtown."

Audra nodded. She and Cole had not spoken since they began their search.

"Did she have a jacket with her, Audra?"

"Yes," was all she said. She didn't want to irritate her brother any more than she had. Her nails dug into the skin of her palms as she sat with her hands fisted, searching diligently out the car window.

"Good. I wouldn't want her to be cold if she's outside somewhere."

They were silent again for some time as they drove around, occasionally getting out to check behind fences or other barriers.

"Cole, I need to eat something. I'm sorry. I haven't eaten since breakfast." Audra hated to ask her brother to stop their search for her to eat, but she was starting to feel sick.

"Fine. Sorry, Audra. I wasn't thinking. Will a stop at a convenience store be okay? I don't want to spend too much time away from searching."

"Sure. That would be fine." Anything would have been acceptable to Audra at that point.

Inside the convenience store, Cole asked the girl behind the counter whether she had seen a guy, a woman or a couple within the past few hours.

"A guy in a brown leather jacket came in, bought some cigarettes. He looked about fifty years old or so. Clean cut guy."

"Anyone else?"

"Umm, a guy on a motorcycle. I think he's Jimmy Knox's brother. You know him?"

"No, any women?"

"No, sir, ain't been no women come through since I've been here. I came in at noon today."

Cole asked her to take his phone number in case she did see anyone fitting their descriptions. He showed the cashier a picture of Sara that he had in his phone and paid for Audra's selections before they left.

Just as they were pulling out of the parking lot of the convenience store, Cole's phone rang again. This time it was his father calling to get an update. His father had stayed at the ranch in case they showed up there. While Audra tore open and ate the contents of the pre-packed foods that constituted her dinner, Cole filled his father in on what little information he had, which was basically nothing.

James and J.P. had paired up in J.P.'s truck to search for Sara. They started several miles out of town and were working their way back in.

"We're missing the majority of the area that we're covering out here, J.P. It's mostly all woods."

"I was just thinking the same thing. They could be anywhere in there."

"Well, if we have to we'll arrange a search team to comb the woods. I just hope to hell we find Sara and that won't be necessary."

They continued to search the roads along the woods methodically. But not with much hope.

Sara could feel the deep gnaw of hunger in her stomach. She'd give anything for a hot dog roll. A box of them was stacked on top of another box of which its contents were labeled as utensils. Both were too far out of reach for her short legs. She looked over at Vinnie, asleep sitting next to her on the floor. He had tried to kiss her after announcing his plan to take a nap. He removed the horrid wad of saliva soaked napkins from her mouth and leaned into her. Sara had turned her head away from him. He grabbed her jaw and attempted to pull her face back toward him but managed to make contact with only a small corner of her mouth. Luckily he had been satisfied with that. Unfortunately, he replaced and even replenished the wad of napkins. It was growing dark now. Sara's jacket nipped the cold air in the sunshine of day but certainly didn't keep her toasty warm in the cool night.

William called the police station and spoke to the police chief. Their lack of information and apparent willingness to do no more than 'keep an eye out' appalled him.

"There's been no sign of this Vinnie guy over the past few weeks, William. I think he left the area. I think you're barking up the wrong tree with holding out that it's this Vinnie guy that's got her."

"Why aren't you out there looking for her? No matter who has her."

"It's only been a few hours since she was last seen. I told you, we gotta wait twenty-four hours before she's considered a missing person."

"Look, she's not here. So that makes her missing!" William knew he was getting nowhere. He kept his anger in check. This time. But wasn't sure he was going to be able to do so much longer. He had barely hung up from the call with the police chief when his phone rang. Cole asked if William would meet him in town and take Audra back to the farm with him. She was looking tired, he told his father. Cole wanted to keep looking for Sara but there was no need to drag Audra around any longer this evening.

The hard floor of the concession stand was uncomfortable and would have been even if Sara wasn't almost six months pregnant. She shifted, trying to find a comfortable position. Each time she leaned forward the bindings on her wrists chaffed. A splinter off of the wooden post she was tied to pierced the tender skin of her left buttock as she leaned forward one more time in attempt to scoot into some semblance of a comfortable position. Her reaction to the pain, though muffled by the wad of napkins, was enough to wake Vinnie. He sat up quickly, and Sara turned to look over at him. The gray of his eyes darkened with the flare of his anger. She felt her muscles reflexively tighten in reaction. The first punch to her face knocked the soaked wadded paper napkin gag from her mouth. Sara managed a scream before the second punch knocked her unconscious.

"Cole, just let me keep looking for her with you." Audra winced at the whine in her own voice.

"No. Dad's here, go home with him." His response was terse.

William's car pulled up beside Cole's in the Farmer's Market parking lot where he and Audra were waiting for him.

"I'm not going home…"

"Enough, Audra. Get out!"

Cole had never yelled at her like that and it scared her.

Her wide-eyed reaction followed by a shimmer of tears welling made Cole realize what he'd done. He leaned over and gathered his sister in his arms. Cole needed the contact as much as she did. He rubbed her back soothingly and spoke into her hair. "I love you. You need to go home and rest. Be there with Dad in case Sara comes home. Would you do that for me?" He released her from his hug and wiped at the tears on her cheeks with his thumbs.

Audra nodded, unbuckled her seatbelt and left the car. Cole watched as his father helped his sister into the passenger seat of his car to take her home. He needed to find Sara. All kinds of sick thoughts of what could be happening to her were making him crazy.

Sara let her eyes open to just slits. Her head was wracked with pain, and she didn't know where Vinnie was. She tried not to move, hoping he would think she was still unconscious, but she needed to know where he was. Moving her eyes within the slits of her eyelids caused unbelievable pain. She heard the rustle of him moving before she felt his body snuggle up close to hers. With each jostle his movement caused to her body she felt the sting of the wood splinter moving within her flesh. She swallowed hard. Then she realized that he had replaced the napkin wad. She felt and tasted chunks of dirt that had gathered onto it from being on the floor. She tried not to think about it. She felt the sting of tears behind her eyelids. He snuggled in even closer with one arm around her shoulders and the other he rested on her belly. He slid his fingers into the opening between the buttons of her blouse. A tear slid slowly down her cheek. He began to work at the button. Sara's body began to tremble. Vinnie must have taken her body's trembling as a sign of her excitement. He let out a soft moan. Sara swallowed hard and prayed that Vinnie would stop at unbuttoning the one button.

James called Cole. "J.P. and I are heading back home, bro'. We've seen nothing and aren't going to be seeing much of anything in the dark."

A long sigh was all that James received as a response from Cole.

"Come on, Cole. Call it a night and get some rest. We'll start first thing at the crack of dawn tomorrow, okay?"

"James, I just can't give up."

"You're not giving up, Cole. We need the light of day. It'd be different if someone had seen or heard something. Let J.P. drop me off at the farm, then I'll go to your place and stay with you in town tonight. We can get our early start tomorrow."

Cole reluctantly agreed and turned his car in the direction of the little rental house in town. He pulled into the driveway and parked his car, then turned off the ignition. He had no energy to even get out of his car. He let his head fall onto the steering wheel, and he closed his eyes. *Where is she?* Cole couldn't stand the thought that she may be being mistreated or hurt. He couldn't think about any other things that she could be going through. *God no, not my sweet Sara. Please let her be safe.*

The headlights of James' car shined blindingly in Cole's rearview mirror. Cole lifted his head off the steering wheel and got out of his car to meet his brother. James went to his brother and gave him a hug.

"I'm so sorry, bro'. This is a true nightmare. We'll find her."

Cole hoped his brother was right—that Sara would be found, and soon. Cole unlocked the house's front door and let James in. They both tossed their sets of keys onto the small table in the foyer.

"The bed in the extra bedroom is made up. Towels are in the hall closet."

"Thanks." James walked into the kitchen. As he opened the refrigerator door, he asked, "Got any beer?" He grabbed two bottles and found his brother sitting in the living room. James handed Cole one of bottles. They sat in silence for a long moment.

"Why? Why is this happening?"

"Doesn't make any sense."

"Why can't I just live a fucking normal life? Find a girl, get married, have a kid. That's all I want. She's so sweet, James. Why would someone do this to Sara? She doesn't need this. She's pregnant, for crying out loud."

"Cole, we'll find her. Sara's gonna be fine." James hoped that he sounded confident.

"What's he doing to her, James? Where is she and what's he doing to her right now? Is she still alive? Has he killed my wife and child?"

James got up from his chair in the living room and went to kitchen. He returned with a bottle of bourbon and two glasses. James poured some into each glass and handed one to Cole. When Cole finished that glass, James filled another for his brother. Cole didn't sleep much that night but at least the bourbon had helped calm his nerves some.

Cole and James had begun searching the wooded area, starting nearest to where the Farmer's Market building was downtown. The sun had just barely come up when they had started out that morning. The brothers had been walking in the woods for two hours when Cole's phone rang. He answered.

"Officer O'Malley here. Cole, we got a possible sighting at a rest area off the highway. One of other officers is headed there now. Just wanted to let you know and tell you we'll get back to you as soon as we have some info."

"Where? Which rest area? How far out of town?"

"We'll be getting back to you, Mr. Becker, as soon as we have some info." The officer hung up.

"Bastard! Dammit, he hung up."

"What's going on?" James asked.

"Possible sighting, but the damn officer won't tell me which rest area off the highway."

"Cops are going out there now?"

"Yeah."

"Let's get a cup of coffee at the diner. Then we can figure out what we're doing from there."

About an hour later, Cole and James were met by Henry, Tommy, and J.P. at the diner. Several opinions of what the next step should be were voiced among the men. All talk stopped when Cole's phone finally rang.

"Okay, thanks." Cole ended the call. "Dead end. It wasn't them."

The group let out a collective sigh of disbelief. Henry stood from his seat to pace. Rounds of curses were spit out across the diner's table.

"Back to the drawing board, come on guys, let's figure this out." J.P. took charge and soon everyone was back on the streets, and in the woods, looking for Sara.

Sara was alone in the concession stand when she woke up. She had slept sitting up tied to the post, in the same position she had been in since Vinnie brought her here the evening before. She considered herself lucky when Vinnie did no more than fondle her breasts last evening. After the night of being tied to a post, Sara's neck ached and one buttock had become numb. And still, her head hurt. She could feel the pain of bruising on her face. It was still dark, though dawn was threatening the day. She unfortunately had little time to devise any plan upon realizing that she was alone when Vinnie returned to the concession stand.

"I've got us a car, Rachel." Vinnie was excited. He spoke quickly in hushed tones.

Sara had to assume that he meant he'd stolen a car. Immediately she began to wonder where he would take her. She knew that if he managed to take her away in the car her chances of being found were going to be even more limited.

"And some food."

Vinnie produced a donut from inside his jacket. It had a small bite taken from it, and Sara figured it hadn't been Vinnie who had taken the bite. He probably found it in a garbage can.

"I'm gonna take these napkins out of your mouth, Rachel, so you can take a bite. Be a good girl and don't scream, okay? 'Cause I'll just punch your fuckin' face if you try." He did as he said and removed the napkins, quickly replacing the wad with the donut.

Sara tasted the sweet cinnamon sugar coating the donut. It seemed so out of place, almost surreal. She knew that she would not be getting anything more or better than this offering, so she bit down into it. The fried outside was stale and tough to bite through. Sara chewed off a piece and worked at it while Vinnie watched her carefully. His arm was cocked into position, ready to punch if Sara tried anything. She was granted two more bites before Vinnie replaced the napkin wad and finished eating the donut.

It had been two days since Sara disappeared. By the third, Cole felt like he just couldn't take much more. Life was throwing one fast ball after another with no time to recover between pitches. He spent his days walking through the wooded areas around town and nights demanding of no one in particular answers, and the return of his wife and child. How had it come to this? He was walking through hell. All he could think to do was take a shower and go start looking again.

Cole stepped out of the bathroom after showering. James set two foam cups onto the kitchen counter, then took sugar packets and plastic stirrers from the inside pocket of leather jacket. He placed those on the counter next to the coffees. He picked up one cup, removed the lid and looked at Cole over the top of the cup as he took a sip.

"Anything new since I last talked to you?"

"No." Cole turned and went to his room. He came back into the kitchen a moment later wearing jeans and T-shirt. Cole took the other cup of coffee from the counter and began to remove the lid to add sugar. The phone rang. James answered it, then handed it to Cole.

"Officer O'Malley here. Cole, I just wanted to touch base with you. Any word from your wife on your end?"

"Nothing. I've been walking through the wooded areas around town but with no luck. And you've not found anything either, huh? No leads."

"No, only thing we've got was a stolen vehicle yesterday. Found it this morning parked near the public athletic fields. It was only missing for a few hours. Must have been some kids going for a joy ride."

"Well, thanks for the update. I guess we'll be in touch again."

"Sure thing. Talk to you later."

Cole ended the call and returned to fixing his coffee.

"I take it there's no news," James said.

"Nothing related to Sara. Just a stolen car reported last night that the cops found a few hours later parked in town by the athletic fields."

James was quiet for a moment. Cole sipped his coffee. "Cole, the cop said they found a stolen car parked out in the middle of town? Just a few hours after it had been stolen?"

"That's what he said. What of it?"

"It's Vinnie's get-away car. I bet you that Vinnie stole a car in the night and parked it where it would be convenient to easily get Sara into it and take off. Only, the cops got to finding it before he could get her into it and take off. They're still here somewhere. Somewhere in

194

town. Let's go!"

Cole grabbed his phone and cup of coffee, then followed James out the door to the driveway. James told Cole to get into James' car. Even though they were downtown, it would be faster to get to the athletic fields by car, and they would have the car with them if Vinnie tried to make a break for it and run. Cole called his father at Bridgeton Pass on the way to the athletic fields. William told Cole that he would send all available hands into town to help out.

Both brothers' hearts beat wildly as they quickly made their way out of James' car once he had parked in front of the athletic fields.

"I'll go this way," James pointed in one direction, "you go that way."

Cole started his search in the playground, checking inside the wooden playhouse structure. Henry's truck skidded to a stop and parked beside James' car as Cole climbed down the playhouse ladder. Henry and Tommy jumped out and ran to join the search.

The growl of Sara's empty stomach seemed to echo throughout the concession stand. She tried to get Vinnie's attention when she saw that he did not react to her body's clear beg for food. Sara tapped her foot on the floor and waited. He was ignoring her. Bastard. It had been only about two hours since Vinnie had returned with the stale donut, but she was pregnant, and he had given her only three bites. She let her head drop back against the post that she was still tied to and sighed.

"Get ready, bitch. I got that car parked out front. It's before the noon lunch rush, so we're gonna make our way out to the car quietly. You got that, quietly. No one should see us and if they do, we'll be out of here so fast they won't find us." Vinnie stared at her and showed her a crude grin, exposing his rotten teeth. Sara noticed the knife he held in his right hand. The blade was long. Just the sight of it made her feel nauseous. It made her actually shudder. Vinnie continued to stare at Sara. The stillness between them was peculiar. He was enjoying seeing the fear that she was trying so hard to hide.

Sara heard the slamming of truck doors followed by voices. She closed her eyes and wished that the people would find her. Vinnie became anxious when he heard the noises and voices.

"Damn," he said through gritted teeth.

With much effort Sara worked to eject the napkin wad and screamed with everything she had in her. Even while she screamed Sara braced for the blow. Pain quickly followed the shock of being bitten. She was totally unprepared for this method of abuse from her abductor. With his mouth firmly against her neck, he sunk his teeth into her skin. Limited by the inability to use her bounded arms, she tried to writhe so as to dislodge the hold he kept on her with his mouth. He held her body still with his hands on her shoulders. His open mouth stayed in place against her neck. The tip of his tongue extended and with the hardened tip he licked her skin. Quickly, he pulled his lips together tight and sucked hard. Sara continued to try to fight him. Dizziness overcame her, yet she still attempted to writhe and scream.

Footsteps pounded on the hard packed dirt ground outside the concession stand, followed by attempts to break open the locked and barricaded door. Vinnie bit down harder on her neck in response. Sara heard the deep guttural yell that at first she didn't realize had come from her. Shards of glass sprayed across the counter above their heads and onto the floor around them. Someone was still working to get the door open. Vinnie had stopped biting her and was moving beside her, but Sara couldn't see what he was doing. She could hear the remaining broken glass being cleared from the window frame, then someone trying to climb in through the window.

Vinnie stood and turned to face the intruder. "No," Sara yelled when she saw that Vinnie held the knife at his side. "He's got a knife!" she tried to warn whoever was in the window above her. Vinnie gave Sara a swift kick and lunged at the intruder. Glass crunched beneath the two bodies rolling on the floor in front of Sara. She gasped for breath and rode the wave of pain shooting through her stomach. The intruder had managed to grab the wrist of Vinnie's hand that held the knife. Blood dripped down the intruder's arm as he held Vinnie's weapon yielded hand at bay. The tangle that was Vinnie and this cowboy's body stopped rolling. The cowboy had pinned Vinnie beneath him to the floor. A second cowboy had come through the same window. He kicked Vinnie's hand holding the knife with his booted foot, effectively disarming Vinnie of his weapon. The cowboy then pushed the boxes away and unlocked the door. A police officer entered and cuffed Vinnie.

The cowboy that had been holding Vinnie to the floor knelt before Sara. It was Tommy, one of the hands at Bridgeton Pass Farms.

"Are you okay?" His gaze wandered over Sara, taking account of her injuries. She was moaning.

"Oh God, it hurts so much!" Waves of nausea fell over her with each vice-like gripping contraction. Sara's face twisted into a tight grimace in response to the pain. Tommy shouted for someone to bring him the knife that Vinnie had been holding. Henry, the second cowboy who had come through the window, retrieved the knife from where it lay on the floor and gave it to Tommy. Henry held Sara's wrists steady while Tommy used the knife to cut the ropes that had been binding her hands. It would take a few minutes for Sara's body to help her stand. Her muscles had become stiff and sore from sitting in one position for so long. She was also having painful contractions. The two cowboys standing over her then stepped aside and Cole walked in between them to Sara.

"Oh, Sara!" He dropped to his knees and held her gently in his arms. He kissed her forehead. He could see that the right side of her face and the bite mark on her neck were beginning to swell and there was evidence of bruises as well. She was still shaking. Cole helped her to stand slowly. She gasped as a pain tore at the underside of her belly. Cole steadied her in his arms.

"I'm all right," she said weakly.

At the doorway, Cole helped Sara step down from the concession stand floor to the ground below. That was when he noticed the abraded, reddened skin around her wrists. He looked around for a police officer. He wanted one of the officers to question Sara quickly so he could take her to the hospital. Suddenly, James appeared and helped to steady Sara from her other side.

"There's an ambulance here for her," he said, pointing in the direction of the vehicle. One of the attendants was bandaging Tommy's arm. The other was bringing a stretcher to Sara.

Sara woke to the sensation of soft lips pressing against her forehead. She opened her eyes to see Audra's face hovering over hers.

"I'm sorry. I didn't mean to wake you."

Sara looked over to see Cole beside Audra. He smiled at Sara.

"Morning, beautiful. How are you doing?"

Audra stepped out of the way to allow Cole room to lean in and kiss his wife.

"Okay, I guess." She managed a slight smile. She felt groggy and then slowly she began to become aware of the pain throughout her body.

Cole noticed her wince. "You were given medicine to help you sleep. The nurse said that you can also have something for pain, if you want it."

Sara nodded. "I think I need something. My stomach hurts, where Vinnie kicked me." She pushed the nurse call button on the side rail of her bed, then asked Cole, "Is the baby okay?"

"They did tests," he told her. "The baby looks fine, they said."

"Thank God. What happened? Why…?"

Cole saw Audra's body stiffen. He could practically feel her tension and guilt. He looked at Audra, then turned back to Sara. Audra quickly left the room. He knew she was crying again. He hoped that James and their father would comfort her. They were waiting in a lounge in the hallway outside of Sara's hospital room. Cole turned his attention back to Sara.

He explained that Vinnie apparently had a history of psychological illness. He was currently in jail and would receive treatment there.

"According to the police, it's unclear whether this history of psychological illness was present before or because of the tragic death of his girlfriend almost one year ago. Vinnie had been living in Mississippi with his girlfriend at that time. She was apparently pregnant with Vinnie's child when she overdosed on heroine. It was unclear whether she had overdosed on purpose or by accident. Vinnie has apparently been wandering since. Unfortunately, Sara, you look similar enough to his deceased girlfriend, Rachel, that Vinnie had apparently believed you to be the pregnant girlfriend that he lost."

Sara shuddered at the explanation. "I thought maybe it was something like that. He kept calling me Rachel."

"I'm so sorry this happened to you, Sara. I should have kept you with me, kept you safe."

"What more could have been done, Cole? I was a prisoner at your sister's house as it was. How long could that have gone on for?"

"You could have stayed in my office or at least in the administrative building."

"And do what all day?" She closed her eyes briefly and sighed. "There wasn't a real solution for this." Sara began to wonder whether he blamed Audra. He had mentioned that he should have kept her in his office. Did he feel that he should have kept her in his office because he believed Audra had failed to keep her safe? It would kill her if Cole felt that he had entrusted his sister with her care but she'd failed him. She thought of the way Audra had abruptly left the room when she asked what had happened. Sara turned to him. "Cole…"

She was interrupted by a nurse entering the room to check on her. "Do you have any pain?" the nurse asked.

"Um…" Sara, still troubled by what may be going on between Cole and Audra, tried to focus on the nurse's question. "My belly hurts, and my neck and face." She touched her face gingerly, feeling the swelling there. "And my butt," she added.

The nurse handed Sara a pill and a cup of water. "This is for your pain. Have you had any more contractions?"

"No."

"Good. It looks like the pain in your belly is just a muscle pull. So, don't worry about that. You had tests last night. Those straps on your belly are a fetal monitor. The baby is fine," the nurse explained.

"Great!" Sara exhaled and looked at Cole for support.

"Your face is bruised and you're sporting a black eye. Nothing broken, though." She paused. "The IV you've got has antibiotic in it. We removed the splinter of wood from your butt cheek. That will be sore for a bit. We put some antibiotic on that and the bite on your neck and covered them with bandages. In a few hours, you'll be due to have those wounds checked and re-dressed." Sara noticed that some of the antibiotic ointment had been put on her wrists as well.

"Thank you," Sara said as the nurse left. Sara would be able to leave later today if all remained well.

But all did not remain well. Sara had a contraction just before noon. She immediately called for a nurse. She checked the monitor strapped to Sara's midsection as well as the one on the wall over her bed. She took Sara's pulse and checked her IV.

"Any more contractions?"

"No."

"Everything looks just fine, Sara. Try to relax and rest some."

Cole was concerned, his wife did not appear to be comforted with the nurse's assessment.

"Call her doctor, please. I'd like him to come in and examine Sara. I'd also like to speak with him." The nurse told them that she would page the doctor, then left the room.

Cole brushed the hair off of his wife's forehead. "Do you still have pain, Sara?"

"Yes. And it figures, she just left and now I have to go to the bathroom." Sara pushed the button on her bed rail to call for the nurse again. She wasn't too quick to answer this time but eventually the nurse came. Managing the fetal monitor and IV pole, the nurse also helped Sara onto the toilet. Sara gasped when she stood and saw blood in the toilet. Her gaze shot to the nurse, who paled and appeared to be struck with panic.

Quickly, Sara was assisted back to the bed. The doctor arrived shortly thereafter to examine her. Tests were ordered. Then he met with Sara and Cole at her bedside.

"All her tests and the monitors show that everything is

normal. Some women do have some spotting during their pregnancy. It's not unusual and doesn't necessarily mean that there is a problem. I can only explain the random contraction as probably due to anxiety, given all that you've been through."

Sara and Cole listened, nodding their heads while taking in all the information. "But why does she still have pain? Something just doesn't seem right. Could we be missing something?"

"Truly, everything looks just fine. The pain is most likely from the kick she received to her abdomen, some soft tissue bruising. I would like her to stay overnight, though, so that we can monitor her for the next twenty-four hours."

Sara and Cole exchanged worried glances.

"Are you okay with that, Sara? Will you stay overnight to be monitored?"

"Yes. May my husband stay with me overnight?"

The doctor smiled. "I'll have the nurse get your husband set up for his stay with you tonight."

They thanked the doctor.

Cole sat on the edge of Sara's bed and wrapped his arm around her. "I want you to come home but thank you for staying. I almost lost you, and I just want to be sure you're okay." He buried his face into Sara's hair and held her tight. "I couldn't live without you, Sara."

Sara turned her face to kiss Cole gently on his lips. "I want to go home too. But you'll be here with me. We'll go home tomorrow."

For much of the evening, Cole sat by Sara's bed, holding her hand. His family had left earlier in the day when Sara had appeared to be doing well and everyone thought she would be going home. He watched Sara sleep. Looking at her bruises and wounds tore him apart. Her face was swollen from where she had been punched. *This guy has punched my wife, multiple times and in the face. What kind of man does that? And what kind of man kicks a pregnant woman in the stomach? It doesn't make sense. Especially if this guy has believed that the baby was his.* But, it didn't have to make sense. The man was not in his right mind. Nevertheless, that knowledge didn't make Cole feel any better.

Sara stirred in her sleep. Muscles in her right hand and left leg twitched. Cole sat up in his chair by her bed. She was dreaming, more likely having a nightmare. Shaking her gently, he woke her. When she opened her eyes, Cole saw the terror behind them. It scared him but didn't let it show. He spoke softly to his wife to calm her. The terror didn't appear to fade. Instead, Sara seemed to be getting more anxious. She let out a scream filled with fear and pain. She squeezed Cole's hand so hard he thought it may break. Cole watched as her body jerked and sobbing screams bellowed from deep within her. Her head came off the pillow several times between screams and moans. She pulled the bed sheets away and sat up. Cole felt like he was walking through hell again. The bed and Sara were soaked in blood. Her hands were now covered in blood. She held them out as if trying to get rid of them, wanting someone to take them away from her.

The door to her room crashed open. Cole was escorted away from her bedside as two nurses and a doctor crowded around her, checking monitors, injecting medication into her IV and then he couldn't see what they were doing anymore. There were too many people in the way. He was made to leave the room, taken to a small waiting area. Eventually, he was told that she had been rushed to surgery to identify where the bleeding was coming from and to control it. Sara's blood pressure had dropped dramatically from the loss of blood putting her and the baby at risk. She was in shock and they hoped, he was told, they could save the baby.

Cole dry scrubbed his face. He listened to the sound of his breathing. It was something to do. He sat in the hospital waiting room. He didn't want to be here. Waiting. He told his father he didn't want anyone to come to the hospital and wait with him. What could they do? It would just drive him crazy to have someone else sitting in the waiting room waiting. Waiting to find out if his wife would be okay. Waiting to find out if his unborn child would live. Waiting to find out how much more fucking hell he would have to live through. He was only twenty-six and he'd lost his mother, helped raised his siblings, nursed his grandparents until their deaths, supported the love of his life through nursing her own mother until the old woman finally died, and now this. A stalker tormented then abducted his pregnant wife, beat her and left him wondering whether his wife would ever wake up again or if his child had been murdered. Would they have to go to the murder trial? How long would that last, being reminded over and over of their loss? How would they deal with seeing Audra still pregnant then enjoying her child? He didn't want this. He didn't want to sit in a waiting room. He didn't want to live with all these feelings, memories and fears. He didn't want to feel sorry for himself and angry at his sister. He didn't want his wife to have pain or live the rest of her life with memories of terror and abuse. But none of what he wanted mattered. It just was. So, he waited.

Dr. Morrison, middle-aged, dressed in scrubs, obviously just having come from surgery came down the hall toward Cole. The doctor stopped at the nurses' station. He put his hands on the counter and forward leaned on his arms. He said something. He looked at Cole, then back at the nurse he was speaking to. *Just get down here and tell me.* The doctor nodded and thumped the counter with his fist, then turned and walked toward Cole again. Finally, he reached Cole and stood before him.

"Your wife and baby are doing well." He talked more about the procedure and what to expect, but Cole heard none of it. His body and mind shut down. The switch had been thrown, and he was given the okay to finally take a deep breath. Sara and the baby were fine.

Two weeks later...

The room was dimly lit. A lamp with a small wattage bulb sat on a side table next to a row of standard office arm chairs. There were no windows in the room. Cole chose one of the chairs to sit in, then waited. This was where he was instructed to come. There was no one here, so he waited.

"Cole?" a soft voice said from across the room. He hadn't heard the door open.

"Yes," he replied and assumed that she wanted him to go into the office with her. So he stood. He looked at the floor. It was carpeted. The pattern was primarily squares, blocks actually. He would go with her into her office.

Her office had a window. And a plant. One of those ivy kind that grow long and trail. He wondered if it had a destination or if it just grew in that direction at random. His wife had been stalked, abducted, beaten. Tortured really. And their daughter's life had been threatened. Before she was even born. Where was he while all this happened? In his office, working. He was supposed to tell this woman with the trailing ivy plant these things about his life. How he felt about what happened to his wife. As if, "One day, my wife went to the Farmer's Market with my sister and was abducted..." was a story to be shared with others. She sat in her hospital bed with blood on her hands. She didn't want the blood on her hands. He was there. He saw it. It was as good as the blood of his baby daughter.

"I have to go," he said calmly. But he didn't stand.

The crumpling sound of the paper bag bothered Audra. She tried to slip the apple and the wrapped turkey and tomato sandwich on wheat bread with light mayo into the bag as delicately as possible. Then she would take some pain medicine and try to sleep off her headache. She didn't usually get headaches. This was odd for her, but she seemed to be getting them more frequently. She placed the bag, lunch for her husband, on the edge of the kitchen counter. He would take it on his way out of the house.

"Want some cereal?" J.P. stood near the kitchen cabinet which housed the cereal bowls ready to get one for Audra if she said 'yes.'

"No, thanks." She sighed heavily.

"Do you have another headache?"

"It's not bad. It'll go away soon." She didn't want her husband to worry. He had plenty of stress. Jericho would be running the first of the major races this season in April. The horse was the best the farm has had for a while. They all needed this horse to win.

"I'm worried about you. You never get headaches and you've have several lately. And you're pregnant." He paused. "You're also harboring a lot of guilt about what happened to Sara. I don't know how to help you with that. I wish I did." He crossed the kitchen to where she was standing and pulled her into his arms.

"I don't know either. I should have been more cautious. I was stupid to bring Sara into town with me."

He stood back to look at her. "Audra, you make her sound like she's a child. Sara is a grown woman and made the choice to get into the car and go with you. And you know that you had nothing to do with her getting hurt by that lunatic."

"I know, but I still can't help the guilt I feel."

J.P. sighed. He felt useless to help his wife. And he needed to get to work. With Cole out of the office more than in it these days, J.P. and James had been working harder to pick up the slack. He bent his knees to bring himself to eye level with Audra. "They don't blame you, darlin', so please stop blaming yourself. It's not doing any good." Her eyes dropped away from his. He slid his arm around her waist and pulled her close to bury his face in her neck. He nipped and kissed below her ear, then whispered, "I'm gonna rub your feet when I get home tonight. Maybe I'll just start there and work my way up."

"Don't say it if you don't mean it, cowboy." She giggled.

"Oh, I mean it." His eyes sparkled when he looked at her just before placing his lips softly onto hers. He slid his lips smoothly across hers, then licked her bottom lip. She let out a low hum. "I've got to go," he said reluctantly, "have a good day."

The contractor was just parking when Sara drove up at the farm's administrative building. William would be meeting with her and the contractor today regarding installation of the kitchen cabinets. Sara hated to keep her father-in-law from his business, but he insisted on being at this meeting. Cole would be seeing a therapist today, for their first visit, so he would not be available to discuss cabinet placement. He wasn't able to focus on much of anything recently. And neither was Sara really. Maybe they should suspend completion of building her and Cole's house. William had suggested it, but Sara wanted to try to keep everything going on in her life as normal as possible. She really felt that doing that would be very important to healing after the trauma she'd been through. She had seen a therapist for a few visits already. It had been helpful, but she seemed to be doing better than Cole had with dealing with trauma. Her therapist suspected that Cole blamed himself, and possibly even partially blamed his sister, for what had happened. Sara, through her actions and reactions during the trauma, had some measure of control over what had happened to her. That little bit had helped her to accept and begin healing before Cole had been able. Nonetheless, everyone processes and deals with stressors differently. Sara was sure that she and Cole would get through this.

* * *

The woman, his therapist, didn't say anything. She just waited for Cole to decide what he was going to do. He didn't move from his seat, though he had said he needed to leave. So, they talked.

* * *

One thing Sara couldn't do while still living in Casey's little house in town was hang laundry. She was surprised how easy it was for her to continue to live there after she'd been released from the hospital. Sure, she looked over her shoulder way too often and was sometimes afraid to stand directly in front of a window. But she kept reminding herself that she was safe now. Eventually, she figured, these things wouldn't bother her anymore.

The major races, the Spring Race season, was over. Jericho was the big winner in two out of three of the races. Bridgeton Pass farms had something to be very happy about. Their wins meant they would be in the black and they also meant that the contract to breed Jericho with Myrna Bingham's mare, Dare to Win, went through. J.P.

could breathe easy for a little bit. Audra was feeling well and their baby was growing. J.P. was so proud. He couldn't wait to be a dad. If only he could help Audra with the feelings of guilt that she still harbored, he would feel better.

J.P. leaned back in the conference room chair. James sat across from him, and they waited for the meeting to start. Still missing were Cole, William, and Melissa.

"Crap. I forgot to bring a pen. Got one I can borrow, James?" J.P. asked.

"Sure." James pulled a pen from his briefcase. Cole entered carrying a notepad and a pen. He squeezed behind the chair J.P. was leaning back in to take a seat on the other side of J.P. James slid the pen across the table. It eluded J.P.'s grasp and slid off the edge, hitting Cole's thigh.

"Come on! Grow up, you two!" Cole snapped.

"Easy, bro'," James retorted.

"Shut up, James! I'm sick of your games. You two think that you can just lounge around all day and laugh. I'm up to my ears in work. I'm trying to build a damn, fuckin' house. Never mind that I have to worry about Sara because of your wife." With that last statement, Cole looked directly at J.P.

"Enough." William stood still in the conference room doorway. Melissa shuddered, standing behind him holding a stack of papers, her notebook, a pen, and a cup of coffee. He turned to Melissa and asked her to reschedule the meeting, then entered the conference room and closed the door.

"I don't know what was going on in here before I stepped into the doorway but whatever it was is finished. This is a professional place of business. Cole, you've got a mountain on your back at the moment, but when has your brother or J.P. ever let you down? Huh? Never. Not in work. Not in life. So, what's going on?"

The room was quiet for a long time. Cole's face was hard. His pain was obvious. "I've got a lot on my mind, Dad."

"And that gives you the right to speak to your co-workers and family like that?"

"I'm sorry, James and J.P." Cole assured eye contact with each man as he apologized.

William nodded. "They have taken some of your work…"

"I know they have, Dad. I was out of line. And on top of it, I've never even thanked them for their help. I'm sorry for being a shit-head lately."

James leaned over and fist-bumped Cole. He felt for his brother making all these apologies in front of an audience.

William cleared his throat. "Now," he focused on Cole and J.P. sitting next to each other, "I will say it once. There is nothing that Audra did that you can blame her for."

Cole turned away, his eyes welling up with tears.

"I know you're hurting, Cole. You have every right to be angry. But Audra is not who you're angry at. God dammit, Cole, she's your sister." In a lower voice, William added, "The one you helped raise."

Cole tightened his jaw. He was angry that he had been blaming Audra and himself for not taking care of Sara. He had made a promise, vowed, to take care of Sara. How had all of this happened? He didn't know, but his father was right. Audra was not to blame for anything that happened. He needed to tell her that. But first, he apologized to J.P. for blaming his wife.

May 2013

The cushions on the couch in Casey's house were getting old. Cole rearranged the throw pillows several times, trying to get comfortable on that couch. For the moment, he was fairly comfortable, so he laced his fingers together behind his head and closed his eyes. It was a beautiful Saturday afternoon. The warm sun through the living room windows felt good on his face and chest. He began to feel sleepy.

Sara stopped short when she got to the living room and saw Cole lying on the couch. His eyes were shut and he looked relaxed. She hadn't seen him relax since the trauma back in March. A tear formed in the corner of one eye. She wanted this so badly for Cole, for him to just be able to relax even for a short while. So, she leaned against the wall and watched him. She loved him so much. They'd been through a lot, too much, together. They also managed to make it through together. He was a good husband. Sara knew he cherished her. She knew that when she walked into a room full of people Cole saw only her. He always made sure that Sara knew he loved her, even through the hardest of their times together. All that they wanted for each other was to be together to love one another.

He repositioned his hips but didn't open his eyes. Doing so tugged his jeans a little lower, exposing the top of the waistband of his tighty whiteys. He was so sexy lying on the couch with hands under his head, bare chest, worn jeans tugged low, and no shoes. God, she loved him. He knew her every sweet spot and visited them often. He was always touching her in some way, keeping them connected as much as he could.

"Hey, gorgeous." She hadn't noticed him open his eyes. Deep chocolate brown eyes stared at her, half hooded.

"I love to look at you." She cocked her head to one

side, never taking her gaze from him. "You look so relaxed today, Cole." She paused. "It's nice to see. How do you feel?"

"I feel more like my old self. Come sit with me." He sat up and patted the area on the couch cushion that he left open for her between his legs.

Sara crossed the room and sat on the couch with her back against his chest. He circled his arms around her and buried his face in her hair.

"My sweet angel."

She snuggled closer.

"I had a long talk with Audra," he said. "I know she's not to blame. I was angry. It's not something I'm proud of, having blamed my sister. Not something I ever thought I'd be capable of."

"Some situations make us do things we never thought we would," Sara offered in support.

"Yeah."

"When did you have this conversation with her?" Sara asked.

"About a month ago. I've had to think about it before I could talk more about it."

"Are things between you and her better now?" she asked tentatively.

"Yes."

"I'm glad."

"Me too," he said.

Sara squeezed her arms tight against his arms that circled her.

"Sara?"

"Yes."

"There are some thoughts that I have, and I think maybe you share some of these, that scare the hell out of me. Can we talk about them, because I want you to know that I'm going to try to do my best to work through them, but I'm afraid I might not do so well or even fail you because of them?"

Sara turned her body to face her husband. "Please, tell me."

Cole felt the pieces being put back together. Not quite whole again yet. But definitely, things were improving. Sara helped him to do this. He would be so lost if he didn't have her with him through this. He cradled her face gently in his hands and leaned toward her to place a soft kiss on her lips. Then leaned back again to look at her. "You are my everything, Sara. You always have been. I've been drowning lately, and feeling guilty that I haven't been there for you. How cowardly is that? I should be the one helping you."

"Shhh…we're in this together. We have each other and we're strong together." She brushed a piece of hair from his forehead. She could tell there was more that Cole wanted to talk about. "What else is bothering you?"

"We haven't had sex since all this happened. There was the time you needed to heal from the surgery, and I wasn't in a very stable frame of mind anyway then. I want to give you the time you need. But I also miss you, Sara. I still want you. Just let me have you again."

"Take me." They looked at each other for a long moment. "Please, Cole."

He held her close.

"I'm yours, Cole. Forever."

Cole's dark period was coming to an end. The hard shell that had formed around his heart had been breaking apart. The more his tender self beneath became exposed the more he realized he needed Sara. He would have waited if she had said that she still needed time. But she hadn't, and he needed to be deep within her. It was Saturday afternoon and over the next few days they would be moving into the new home they had built. Packing and moving could wait. Now, he carried his wife into their bedroom. He set her down on her feet beside the bed and lifted her dress over her head. Her feet had been bare. She stood in a matching white lace bra and panties. His angel. Sweet Sara. He popped the buttons of his jeans and removed them along with those sexy tighty whiteys he had on underneath. He kissed her belly and up between her breasts to her neck, stopping there to nuzzle the small dip there. Then he stood before her, cupped her face with his hands and landed a hard, solid kiss on her lips. He couldn't slow down, go easier. He suddenly needed her more than he could imagine, but he didn't want to scare her.

"Are you okay? Did I scare you? I lost my head for a moment there."

"I'm fine. Thank you for being concerned, but just take me. I know it's you who's touching me, and I want it."

"Hot damn. I don't think I can be gentle, angel." He lifted her and placed her in the middle of the bed. "But don't let me hurt you. Okay?" The fire in her eyes told him she wanted him to stop talking and give it to her. So, he did.

Cole knelt in front her as she lay on her back. He draped her legs over his thighs, then leaned forward to kiss her. While sucking in on her bottom lip, he reached down to feel the wetness between her legs. He groaned at how wet she was just before thrusting into her. She called out his name and arched her back. Her breathing grew heavy and more erratic.

He pulled back and groaned as he pushed back in, slowly this time. "You feel so good."

"It's so good. Take me hard, fast. Please."

He kissed her lips and swiped his tongue along hers, then sat back, grasping her hips for leverage. It felt so good to be where he was, deep, warm, and tight. He held her hips and pushed hard into her several times. He could feel her muscles tightening around him, she was close. He would be right behind her. Her body writhed, then straightened as she let out cries of pleasure. Her cries and the feeling of her tight body writhing around his shaft drove him to the edge. He threw his head back, eyes closed tight, and released into her. He pulled out and lay next to her on the bed so he could scoop her into his arms. "Are you okay?"

"Very much so. God, I missed you." She kissed him.

"I love you, Sara. So very much," he said between kisses. He already wanted her again.

By Tuesday afternoon Cole and Sara had moved their meager belongings into their new house. Furniture would begin to be delivered as early as Friday. The house was a colonial with four bedrooms, room for their family to grow. Audra stood in the middle of the living room, sizing it up. The house looked so big without furniture in it, she thought. She imagined a couch, some chairs, and a coffee table in the room. There would still be plenty of room for ride-on toys and building blocks.

"What are you grinning about?" J.P. walked up to her and kissed the top of her head. Since she and Cole had talked and agreed that Audra was not to blame for what had happened to Sara, Audra's headaches disappeared. J.P. wrapped his arms around her waist. At seven months pregnant she had no waist really. J.P. didn't mind that he had to slide his arms under her swollen breasts in order to be able get his arms around his wife to pull her in close and hold her.

"I was just imaging this house full of kids and toys, a new kind of everyday life."

"Mmm...and not a bad place to live it." J.P. let go of Audra and leaned around to look at her face. "I felt that kick!" His elation with having felt his child move within

215

his wife never faded, no matter how many times he felt it. And Audra was warmed by his reaction every time. He whispered "I love you," as he leaned in to kiss her.

"Oh, you guys are great help." Cole teased as he walked in on J.P. and Audra in the living room. Cole carried a large box and set it down on the living room floor. "Come on, it's Moving Day." He attempted to rouse some enthusiasm into the task. Audra rolled her eyes at her big brother.

With little that she and Sara were able to help with, Sara took Audra on a tour of the house. Audra marveled at how everything was shiny and new but thought how she preferred the comfort of the small house's furnishings, worn with memories of family. Cole and Sara's house had plenty of natural light, lots of storage space and several modern amenities, like a dishwasher. Audra admired the wainscoting in the living room and dining room. The sunny yellow kitchen was a reflection of Sara's personality. It had plenty of space for several little cooks to help. In one corner there was even a red step-stool for those little cooks to stand on someday so they could reach the countertops. Audra smiled at Sara when she noticed it. She knew Sara was looking forward to having little cooks helping in the kitchen. The second floor had a master and three bedrooms. They had left the walls in the three bedrooms white, Sara explained, to be decorated according to the occupant's personality, as they arrived. The master bedroom was a modest size with its own bathroom. Cole had assured that a king sized bed had been delivered before they moved in. He said he could do without a living room couch right away, Sara told Audra, but not a bed. It was a beautiful shaker style frame, the light honey color complimented by the soft green walls. There was a definite sense of serenity in the room. But it was the cool gray-blue color of the living room walls that Audra liked best. She wondered if it was the persistent heat she felt with being pregnant that made her prefer that room.

Casey took the opportunity to take a break from carrying boxes to join Sara and Audra unloading items in the kitchen, while still appearing to be helping. She smiled at the two other women bustling about all the while working around each other's protruding bellies. "This family's tapestry is getting bigger and more beautiful all the time," Casey thought out loud.

Audra stopped removing glassware from the box in front of her. Sara stopped placing containers of cooking herbs and spices in the rack. They each looked at Casey with interest. Casey took their interested looks as a collective desire for her to expound on the thought. "When I first stepped foot onto Bridgeton Pass property to care for Audra's wounds I didn't realize that I had become a thread in this family's story. It's a wonderfully beautiful tapestry, rich in colors and texture."

Sara pulled a chair away from the kitchen table to sit. Audra simply said, "Go on, please."

"Well, I feel that I've been welcomed, woven, into this family. I've learned so much about the family and all the different personalities, choices made, directions taken, that sort of thing. It's like studying a tapestry, 'reading' the story it tells, and also watching it continue to be made." Casey felt the need to be somewhat cautious talking about the family at such a personal level.

"J.P. had likened our relationship to a tapestry. This was a few years ago." Audra recounted the memory.

"Really?" Casey was surprised. "How interesting."

"If there really were a tapestry of this family's history, I couldn't imagine how large it would be!" Sara exclaimed.

"And how colorful!" Audra added.

Casey returned to unpacking a box of dry goods. As

she placed the items onto different shelves in the pantry, she thought how humbling it had been to not only be able to watch but also to actually be a part of the Becker family's story as it was being woven.

William went to the kitchen in search of a cold drink and a bit of a reprieve. He was feeling his age with all the manual labor. It was disturbing to think how hard he used work in the barn and now he would never be able to do that work if he tried. The women looked up from their tasks as William entered the kitchen. "Can a working man get a cold drink, by chance? And one for each of his co-workers?"

"Oh, my." Sara was embarrassed for not having offered them anything to drink as they worked so hard. "Of course, let me bring some lemonade out to you on the porch." Given the doors were being left open while moving boxes in, Cole hadn't turned on the central air conditioning. It would be cooler for the men to sit on the porch outside to have their cold drinks. Moments later Sara emerged from the house with a pitcher of lemonade, followed by Casey and Audra helping to carry ice and tall glasses. The women joined the men and sat outside on the porch. James poured, and Tanner helped pass around glasses filled with Sara's homemade lemonade.

J.P. stretched his legs out in front of him as he sat in a wicker chair. "You know, Tanner, this porch would be a nice place to hang out, say, if we needed to change our occasional Friday night drinking-on-the porch venue."

"I agree, cuz. This is a mighty nice spot. And maybe the little lady of the house would even serve us." Tanner knew his chauvinistic comment would get Sara's goat and waited for the fall-out. Tanner received warning remarks from not only Sara but from the other women as well.

"I'd like that," William added. "I could join you when you're on this porch. Since Cole would be out here drinking with us, it would only be polite to have Sara serve us. I mean, we wouldn't rightfully enter her house and help ourselves to the contents of her fridge, right?"

Everyone laughed. The women stuck behind Sara with supportive comments. "If you were anyone but my father-in-law...!" Sara joked. The thing was, Sara thought, she wouldn't mind at all if the men spent the occasional Friday night on her porch with her serving them. She'd rather they be on her porch than at Sully's Saloon.

Cole caught Sara's eye and winked. They would be happy here in their house at Bridgeton Pass.

About the Author
Natalie Alder

I am a sassy 40-something year old. I live in a quiet farming town in New England with my husband of seventeen years and our three rescued cats. After college I facilitated improvement in the physical abilities of children and the elderly then took the opportunity to enjoy my creative side. I love to sew, knit, write...sing and drink martinis (not necessarily at the same time). I write stories about romance. They center on learning about the characters backgrounds, personalities and life circumstances that mold them into who they are and how they love.

Website
http://www.nataliealder.com/
Facebook https://www.facebook.com/AuthorNatalieAlder
Google+ https://plus.google.com/u/0/+NatalieAlder/posts
Goodreads
https://www.goodreads.com/user/show/32799040-natalie-alder
Amazon Author page
https://www.amazon.com/author/nataliealder
Twitter
https://twitter.com/NatalieRomance
          @NatalieRomance
tsu
https://www.tsu.co/NatalieA@NatalieA
Pinterest
https://www.pinterest.com/nataliealder396/
YouTube
http://www.youtube.com/c/NatalieAlder

Other Books by
Natalie Alder

<u>The Tapestry Series:</u>
Crewel Work
Trouble Looming
Woven Interests
Fringe Benefits

Constructing Love

Made in the USA
Middletown, DE
18 June 2016